DISMOUNT NOW SIR!

Terry Clarke

DISMOUNT NOW SIR!

Matador
9 De Montfort Mews
Leicester LE1 7FW, UK
Tel: (+44) 116 255 9311 / 9312
Email: books@troubador.co.uk
Web: www.troubador.co.uk/matador

ISBN 1 905237 05 7

Cover illustration: Terry Clarke

Typeset in 11pt Stempel Garamond by Troubador Publishing Ltd, Leicester, UK

Matador is an imprint of Troubador Publishing

To my wife Margaret
and my friend Jo Richmond
without whom this book would not have seen
the light of day.

Thanks to Terry Halloran and Margaret Clarke for the proof reading, and also to Lorna Cross for agreeing to the use of the two articles by her husband, Roger.

CONTENTS

INTRODUCTION

I had decided to write my stories to explain my early years to my children. It was easier using our computer to set out the layout. I was really enjoying writing, when the roof fell in! Only six stories were completed before my stroke. I was disheartened and desperate. I thought fate was cruel. When I tried writing after convalescing at home, there was nothing. Like my speech, I could not write, obviously they are linked some way, but I didn't know why.

Speech therapy is very good, but naturally it is slow. There are no quick fixes and you have to buckle down to the work. I was grateful to have an hour session a week with hospital therapist Lucy. I accepted the inevitable, there were no more stories. Without my wife Margaret, there was absolutely no chance to re kindle the flame.

I found it was like a brick wall, which I could not climb. Then we were very lucky – Margaret found a therapist, Jo Richmond, and together with Jo's professional guidance we found a glimmer of hope. The hour session of speech therapy each week always provided us with enough work to enable us to do two hours a day on our own. With Margaret pushing me (and a lot of rubbing out), slowly words became sentences and eventually paragraphs. Slowly, very slowly, I completed my first story and tried some others.

One day when Jo was reading my last effort she said, "You should think about publishing your work." This was a can full of worms, I never expected this, but a seed was sown and it was too late...

Around about a year ago, Jo had some "aims and objectives" looking forward three months. Having discussed this we decided to try something much more bold, namely an anthology of forty of my short stories.

Terry Clarke
May 2005

DISMOUNT NOW SIR!

In David Niven's autobiography, *The Moon's a Balloon* there was a chapter about the 1936 film, *The Charge of the Light Brigade* starring Errol Flynn and David Niven. The director of the film was Michael Curtiz. Curtiz was a central European Jew, who had about enough of the English language and no more. In the Charge scene, there was needed some extra rider-less horses. The best that Curtiz could manage was "Bring on the empty horses". Niven found this outrageously funny, he decided it would be a wonderful title for a book.

I was reminded of something, which an old friend said. To say he was over zealous would be under stating the problem. At that time a few neighbours decided we should start a cricket team. The first thing we had to do was finance the kit. We decided to try a Car-Boot sale to get some money. The Cross Keys field had an entrance and an exit, we had to man it as at times it was very busy. Three of us kept the entrances free, Jim Roberts, Peter Watson, and myself.

My over zealous friend was our treasurer and looked after the money, complete with a shoulder bag for the cash. The field being lower than the road, we had a steep incline. My overzealous friend saw a man on a bike riding down this incline. With a commanding stance and a belligerent hand outstretched, said these immortal words, "Dismount now sir!" Well! We were convulsed and could not say anything for a few minutes, the laughter was infectious and uncontrollable. If you had known my over zealous friend you would have known exactly why.

I eventually said to my pals "If I ever write a book its title must be "Dismount now sir".

But this was said as a joke, my change of circumstances and the Speakability motto "I can and I will" made me an author.

SAM GOLLICK

Sam Gollick was a man I never met, and indeed he had departed this life long before I entered it. His story begins with my Aunt Lizzie, who was the next oldest to my Mum in the Hough family. But first my earliest memory of Sam was a large photograph of a soldier with sergeant's stripes on the wall of Aunt Lizzie's tiny house. On another wall was a picture of Pope Pious X11th and both were as part of the wall paper to me as a very young child and I confess at that time, I paid them scant regard. This house was situated in a yard off Kirkgate, behind Andrassy's butchers shop, most of the yard being taken up with the buildings associated with the shop's business.

There was always a get together at Christmas by the whole family at Aunt Lizzie's and we would all crowd into its tiny spaces. We children, my brother Tony and cousins Doreen and Eileen were sent upstairs to play, I suspect to lessen the crowding downstairs. These were happy events and I had great affection for this Aunt, who had at this time buried two husbands and had a hard life without complaint. One memory I have of this time was going through the drawers and playing with the contents, including some First World War medals, of which more later.

Many years later, when only my Uncle Jim remained as the youngest of the Hough family and was living in the flats across from my favourite pub, The Redoubt, I would call and pass the time with him and found I had developed a taste for the past, which he was able to satisfy. Came the day when I asked about the soldier in the photograph and was told by him that it was a picture of Sam Gollick who was Aunt Lizzie's fiancee and that he was responsible for them meeting. It came to pass this way.

At Jim's birth, Lizzie had run to fetch the midwife, a Mrs Gollick and Sam's mother. Sam had then walked Lizzie back home and thus started the courtship. When the World War started in 1914 Sam had joined the KOYLI and gone to France and made sergeant. On a subsequent leave, Jim said "He was my hero and I always followed him about. He was Big Swank and I was Little Swank." And on his return to France, he left Jim his swagger stick, which all senior NCO's had "To look after it until I come home again" Tragically like many others Sam never came home again.

Jim remembers that a sister of Sam's came round to tell the awful news of Sam's death, Jim being a young boy at this time and Lizzie being employed with my mother at Holdsworth's mill was still at work. When she came in from work, her mother (my grandmother) made sure they had their meal before breaking the bad news. Jim remembers Lizzie saying "Oh! I wish I hadn't sent that letter", it seems Lizzie had found a new boyfriend and Sam had been sent a "Dear John". Bad enough I suppose at any time, but in that situation, it must have been awful. Nevertheless, Sam left word that Lizzie was to have his medals (which included a Military Medal). I have often wondered if they were Sam's medals that we played with as children. We now know that the Gollick family have his medals safe. I expect Jim being young himself and the years dulled his recollections. So I still do not know whose medals we played with.

On a whim one day, I called into the Town Hall and asked to see the book of remembrance, where all the names of Wakefield's sons who gave their lives in the war, are listed. I found the name Gollick. Sgt. KOYLI but listed as George. When I later told Uncle Jim of this, he told me that George was Sam's brother also killed in that war, no trace of Sam. This started me on a crusade to make sure Sam was listed in his hometown book of remembrance. First to the Regimental museum at Pontefract barracks, no joy. Then to the Imperial

War Graves Commission, where I obtained all the details, including the fact that Sam was with the London Fusiliers, when he met his death. Armed with this information, I was able to get the listing that he deserved and although it took several months to achieve, it was worthwhile. I hope to see his name later this year when I go to France to view the memorial where his name is carved, as he has no known grave.

Throughout these comings and goings, I kept Uncle Jim informed and was amazed one day when he told me I should have a word with our old neighbour Mary Depledge, who it transpired was Sam's sister as Mary Murgatroyed (Mrs Gollick must have remarried). I had not had any contact with Mary for many years, as we had all scattered after the demolition of our old homes on the Grove, although I had an idea she had moved to Eastmoor. I decided to attempt to find her but realised the futility when I stood forlornly looking about me. A passing lady asked could she help and telling her of my problem, imagine my surprise when she pointed and said "There she is looking at you through that window". I then had the job of persuading Mary that I was who I said I was, she being now an old lady. I spent some time explaining my intentions, but Mary had been too young to ever know Sam, but did tell me that in St Andrews's Church Peterson Road was a plaque to both Sam and George. I was able to see this for myself on the following Sunday, when I called after the service.

I would hope to have some more to add to Sam Gollick's story, when I have been to France

At last the six friends, David and Margaret, Terry and Andy, Margaret and myself, set out to France. Fortunately we had the six People Carrier car borrowed from Steve Hazel, it was just the job.

We enjoyed the journey to Dover and decided to get the faster

"Cat" to Calais. We were soon seeing the sand dunes and struck by the flat land.

Very quickly into Albert, the start of my quest for Sam Gollick.

Albert, previously Ancre (after the river which flows through it) occupied previously by the Germans in 1914, driven out by the French and then the British. As a consequence Albert was very heavily shelled by the Germans in 1918 in their Spring Offensive. The Germans recaptured all of their previously held territory on the Somme. They moved even further westward, taking Albert on March 26th 1918. Sam was killed on 24th April 1918 in this offensive.

Albert was totally destroyed, then rebuilt exactly the same. It is amazing how new houses can look like old ones. We enjoyed a sunny stop and a snack of coffee and beautiful cakes and bread in sight of the Basilica, overlooked by the Golden Virgin holding up the infant Christ.

Now on the road from Albert to Bapaume (N29), immediately we saw dotted about white headstones and "Cross of Sacrifice".

Before I was really prepared, we were at Poziere Military Cemetery and stopped the car. Poziere Military Cemetery was a beautiful place and much better then I expected, the roses and grass could not have been better tended, with all the rows and rows of the white headstones shining in the sun.

But Sam is unfortunately an "unknown grave", so we looked at the panels. David knew exactly where it was and I confess when I saw SGT GOLLICK S. M.M. I had a tear in my eye, even though I was born years after Sam's death.

We found the Military Records Books easily and read Sam's

Pozieres British Cemetery

details. I was surprised to see his address was 21, Charlotte Street, which was very near to my own, on the Grove, over thirty years ago.

I intend to pass all this information to Sam's relatives.

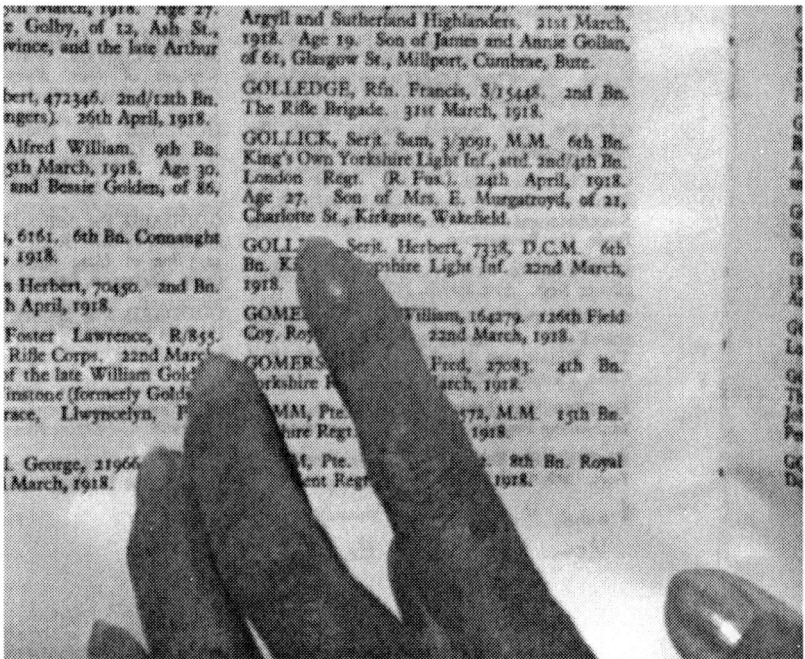

Memorial Register

MEMORIES OF SAINT AUSTIN'S AND BEYOND

I remember my first day at St. Austin's, this may sound a proud boast for a 3yr 7month old infant, but it was also the day my older brother Tony started school on his 5th birthday February 1938. It was also one of the few times my mother told me an untruth, "You are not staying, I am coming back for you". So to all requests 'Drink your milk' or 'Have a nap on this camp bed' my stock answer was 'I am not staying'. The memory is sharp and clear although the animal picture above my cloakroom peg I have long forgotten.

So, here I am at St. Austin's Infants, with Sister Agnes, Miss Lodge, Miss McTernan, a paved playground with a large gate at the Jacobs Well Lane end, with a hole at the bottom where lucky children would have snacks passed through to them, at playtimes by parents.

I have a memory of a collection being made over many weeks, to purchase a statue of a very young looking Christ, costing I think, £16 and being disappointed at its size, expecting something much bigger for that amount of money. It stood I remember in a brick built cupboard on the playground wall.

Another memory is being shown how to do my initials in Plasticine on a board, having first been taught what my initials were.

So up to the Juniors, Miss Raynor, Miss O'Kane, Miss Rawcliffe and Miss Boole who read to us the wonders of *Wind in the Willows*. Miss Moran, Kitty Durkin, Miss Fealy, Miss Harty, determined for us to achieve scholarships, Mrs Ellis,

With my good friend Tony Costello and our teacher
Kitty Durkin in Silgo.

Ken Binks, Johnnie Dewhurst, and the one and only Arthur
Watson, who handled us all with consummate ease and whose
name will always be remembered whenever two or more ex

pupils get together. Then Winnie Powell who left us, her last class to become Sister Winifred of the Heart of Jesus always fair and missed by all she taught. Also her lovely young sister Eileen, who always listened to us, and always laughed with us. Finally the supremely wonderful Sister Maria, who controlled the whole business and who never, appeared to age.

Long after I had left St. Austin's and was doing my National Service in Germany, I wrote to tell her of the local Catholic customs, four candle Advent wreathes etc. I was quite delighted when my younger brother Peter, then still at school wrote and told me that my letter was read out to the whole school at assembly and followed this with a return letter to me, a wonderful lady remembered with affection,

I played rugby for the school, but the stars of the 1948 side had all left but together with Don Nunn, Tony Costello, Andy Quinn, Pete Guilfoyle, Joe Finan etc, we did our best, but sadly, no trophies.

My memory now of St. Austin's is of a place where children meet as pupils and go on through life together as friends, meet on regular occasions, tell the old tales and remember the ones no longer able to keep the appointment.

On a recent holiday in China, when speaking with the various guides showing us about the place, I noticed how often the words "At school we were taught" were used by me, which made me appreciate how well we were taught and that most of it had been remembered. If anyone responsible for that teaching is able to read these words please accept a very grateful, if belated thank you.

WALTER DILL, OUR MAYOR

It was a red-letter day when Wakefield's Mayor and all his retinue came to St. Austin's school. I am sure it was the normal practice at the time for the Mayor to visit every Wakefield school over his period in office. It was an exciting time for the children and a busy time for the teachers.

Somehow I found myself reluctantly chosen to recite a poem. I don't know why I was chosen and I have long forgotten what the poem was called, it didn't matter, I never completed my mission. I know now the poet was Walter-de-la Mare.

The whole business is hazy with time, but my embarrassment is clear and sharp with the pain to this day. I remember two or three classrooms had partitions, which had been rolled back to make one big room, to me it was vast. I could not be more than five years of age at that time. So, there I was with the whole school looking at me. This tiny child.

I stood, the dignitaries sat. The Mayor in red and gold chain and his hat trimmed with fur. The massive mace in my sight. Somehow my fevered brow reacted to all that pomp and circumstance. I took a step towards the Mayor with an outstretched and trembling hand said "Walter Dill, our Mayor".

There was pandemonium, the teachers were laughing, the Mayor's hat fell off, the mace rolled onto the floor, and the children didn't know what to do, so they started laughing too. All the dignitaries were trying to cover their mirth with their hands.

And me! My dismay was complete; I sought solace with abject

misery and floods of tears. If I could have a seen a pit, I would have happily jumped into it.

Over the years and with insight, I suppose most of the people would have had a laugh with me, but at the time it was not quite as I had envisaged. In fact it took many years before I would attempt "Young Lochinvar".

A KNIGHT'S HELMET

If a young boy, walking down the street, took out an imaginary pistol and fired at a passing police car, any adult would assume that he was merely playing a game of cops and robbers. With this in mind, I remembered an occasion in my childhood when a similar happening took place, with different results.

First the lead up to it. The houses in Simpson's Buildings had cellars, the steps of which were protected by railings, from which, I was swinging backwards, missed holding on and fell down to the bottom, was concussed and taken to hospital. Where I was kept in for a couple of days and introduced to sago pudding, like soft ball bearings in milk.

On being released, I had the rest of the week off school, and spent the time on various visits to various relatives, some of whom lived on Thornes Lane. All visits on foot, as this was the early days of the war and no form of transport was available to us. On our way home we called at a small shop, which like all shops at this time, had absolutely nothing on display, goods being kept "under the counter".

My mother and the lady shop owner were deep in a conversation as usual about the war and what Churchill said last night, or what Lord Haw Haw had threatened, leaving me, a very small boy, living in a world of knees and bored. Then I remembered my latest game. By placing my left hand across my mouth and my

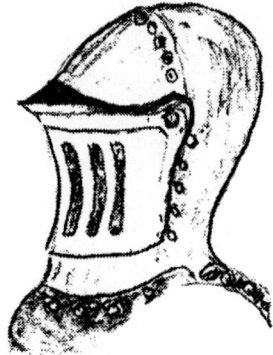

13

right hand across my eyes I could raise the right hand like the visor in a Knight's Helmet and look around for a dragon to slay. This is where the lady in the shop saw my performance and the misunderstanding started. "What's the matter with him? " she asked, " He's fallen down some steps and got concussion" said my Mum. Without reply, the shop woman dived under the counter and surfaced with a 7lb jar of Yorkshire Mixtures. I was completely staggered and couldn't believe my eyes; we hadn't seen these since before Dunkirk. But still more, she screwed off the top, reached in and took out the big fish, always two colours and handed it to me. I couldn't believe my luck and started to suck my fish, I was never sure if this was appeasement, or a bribe, me, being a handy height for leg biting. Either way, we were gradually being guided towards the door. I decided to try my luck and gave the lady a few more raised visors, flapping my hand up and down, this definitely speeded up the process and we were soon out in the street, my mother furious and I sublimely ignorant of what had happened, but disappointed that no more fish were produced.

Except for the memory of the fish and who could forget it, the rest of the episode had left my mind, until 20 years later it came back to me and I saw the funny side of it and realised my mum was a party to that lady thinking that my fall had left me half a lunatic. It should have been obvious to all that I was merely looking for a dragon to slay!

THE GUARD'S VAN

I had a guard's van as a Christmas present, it was totally unexpected. It was brown and with a white top and was boxed, emblazoned on the side the legend was L.N.E.R. and I was delighted. Why did I not ask where the rest of the train set was? I never thought about it, this was wartime and we never had a chance of any thing. So my lone guard's van was the last pre war set. I found later it came from Randal's shop in Kirkgate.

We accepted Randal's was a toyshop, but in fact it was more, it was a newspaper shop, with a dolls hospital, three or four glass cases showing displays of china and glass. On galleried mezzanine level they had a lending library, which my dad used to use, hence my guard's van. Mr and Mrs Randal were a sight to behold. Always immaculate, balding, he always wore white shirt and tie, she, dark clothes and pearls, blonde and red lipped. Their window dressings were famous and as children we ran to if see anything had changed. At special times, like Christmas, there was always a snow scene with plenty of cotton wool. The best time I remember was the whole of the Coronation Procession, with the coach and horses, the Horse Guards and Red Guardsmen lining the route. Again, at Christmas, Randal.s had a grotto and a Father Christmas who gave out presents, (at a cost). This shop was an oasis of tranquillity, the Randal's, their speech was cut glass, nothing like the hurly burly of the Grove.

I remember a Christmas long ago; again it was wartime with all its limits. My older brother, Tony said to me "What if we found a box of fat soldiers in our Christmas Stocking", I could not visualise how fat soldiers got into the box, or how fat they were. I thought they would be blown up like balloons. What he really meant was the pre war lead soldiers; not the thin ones moulded in sand, the only ones you could now get.

I had not thought about these days for over 60 years, we accepted our lot without question and made light of the short-ages, so it does not matter that I could not have the whole of the train set. At least I had my Guard's Van, and I never expected that.

THE SCHOOL DENTIST

I expect there have to be School Dentists, but I am sure all children under seven would ask why? My uninformed school days flowed without too many traumas, a small hiccup when having to see the school nurse, but nothing to write home about.

But the School Dentist! Well, just the hint of the visit filled me with dread. By the time the hint was a fact and the date of the tragedy was named, usually only one month away, but a month of dread. Now older children would tell all the younger ones what transpired. I remembered when I was told all the mysteries of "X" and "F" or "NT" and what it meant.

Now we are queuing, hoping we get the prized "NT" (No treatment) and with it a wide grin of fulfilment. My fellow sufferers were eager to tell me what they got, the wonderful, "NT" or bad enough the "F"(filling) or the dreaded "X"(extraction), it could not be worse, but it was. The man himself was enough to frighten the stout hearted, with his bulging eyes and thick lensed spectacles. I'm sure as like me, all children remember the School Dentist, around about 1930–40.

I remember the time when I was unable to get out of his clutches. It was this way. My older brother Tony had the job of taking me to the surgery. I remember we had found some comics in the waiting room. The white uniformed nurse said "Clarke", whereupon Tony said "Me"? and moved into the surgery. I have to confess a load fell off my shoulders. Was my brother volunteering? Oh no, he was too busy with the comics, to ask what the nurse was saying. However my joy was short-lived, the Dentist saw the error and the nurse quickly pointed her beckoning finger at me, divested of my comics, no escape. The last chapter saw the sentence carried out, the drill, the filling and the pain.

THE GRAND CLOTHING HALL

Having read the Wakefield Express article of "Spires, Towers and Turrets" series. I was immediately reminded of the location of the older shops around this area. I remember in the Bull Ring, the Cable shoe shop was always of good quality. I recall their "slip ons" were so comfortable. In Cross Square was the Crockery, an expensive China and glass shop. Kingswells was a small department store. Also there was Chas. R. Coe's piano and music store. Above all of these stores was The Grand Clothing Hall. This brings back memories of my childhood.

I think it was about 1943–44, my mother arranged to collect me outside St. Austin's after school, to go and choose a new Lumber Jacket, probably now called Bomber Jacket. I would have much preferred to run home to play with my friends. I was always a bit grubby after school, which did not please my Mum, as we were going into town to The Grand Clothing Hall.

Anyway, my mother had taken the jacket from the salesmen, but I was still wearing my old jacket buttoned up. As things were pretty fraught, my mother just dragged off my jacket, when to my horror the picture of Adolf Hitler fell out onto the floor, face up! I had swapped something else for it.

Picture the scene, the salesman wanted to laugh but was frightened to, my mother totally embarrassed and I am not sure what my fate will be!

All the way home, I was thinking of the dire consequences. The best I could expect was to be taken to the Police Station, or the worst to be lined up against the wall and shot, because it was still war time and Hitler was not exactly the flavour of the month.

SIMPSON'S BUILDING, WONDER STREET, WAKEFIELD

I never knew Simpson, but I knew his buildings inside out and back to front, from first moving into the house in December 1938, to eventually moving out in 1953. It was my home address throughout my formative, and easily embarrassed youth and I hated having to give it to strangers.

Simpson's Buildings, comprised of a long narrow yard of seven back to back houses, each having piled on top of each other, a cellar, living room, bedroom and attic, all, I would say from memory about 10ft square.

In number 7 lived Ted and Mary Depledge, Ted, a quiet, easily pleased sort of man, who made models. Mary, a live wire, very much in charge " One of us has to stop smoking Ted, and it's not going to be me!" Mary had lived, as a young girl for a few years with an aunt of mine, before marrying but was already living in number 7 when we arrived, so I suspect, may have had something to do with our getting the rental, I always liked Mary.

Number 6 were the Wards, elderly and eccentric, she always wore running pumps, although I suspect her running days were well behind her. He always appeared in a grubby raincoat buttoned up to the neck, with a large flat cap with it's peak pulled right down allowing only about 4 inches of flesh to be on view. In all the years he was our neighbour, I never saw any more of him than that. The gloom was lifted somewhat by the addition of two young WAAF air women, who lived there for some time. Rumour had it that some time in the 1920's Ward had won £250 decided that was enough, and never worked again, but spent his days mooching round the streets, often in the company of the rag and bone men. There was so little of Ward on view, that I was always reminded of looking at a street post box, especially around the mouth.

I have one childhood embarrassment connected to Ward, of course, these were the war years, with shortages of everything very much the order of the day. On arriving home for lunch one day my mother presented me with a pair of shoes purchased from Ward for the sum of two shillings. These were white and brown in colour with punched holes all over and would have looked right on Bobby Locke, or any other professional golfer but totally wrong on an eight year old boy, who was going to hate wearing them and begged not to have to, but to no avail. As I set off back to school with my correspondent's shoes to my eyes, growing ever bigger because of their colour. Imagine the comments I had to endure from my school pals standing there looking like a miniature Caesar Romero. You can be sure, everything in sight was kicked on the journey to and from school until they were worn out.

Number 5 housed an elderly bachelor, retired plumber, Sam Robinson " Mr Sam". Number 3, the Lovells, Mr and Mrs, three children, Frank (Pewt) Geoff (Minnie) and an infant David, who died an infant, also Harry Foster as a lodger the finest stutterer I ever heard. Who had to kick start any sentence with t'Man, example, "t'Man, it's looking bad over Dewsbury" after rain, and the all-time classic, when the newsreader announced that German raiders were driven off by the RAF dropping their bombs at random," t'Man, I see Rrrandom got it bad again last night."

At Number 2 were the Corfields Joe and Alice, Terry, Donald, and Joseph. Joe Corfield worked full time at the Carlton cinema and was always known to everyone as "Carlo Joe" who attempted to keep us kids quiet at the matinees

Number 1 was occupied by the Robert's family one parent Mrs Robert's, Doreen, Charley and our pal Johnny, who was slim of stature, but a great athlete at any and all ball games. He could almost throw a cricket ball out of sight, and was never allowed to ball his fastest in our games of cricket.

Outside, shared toilets were the order of the day, with our family being lucky to share with plumber Sam the bachelor who ensured we always functioned in the harshest of weather, he being unfortunate of course, to share with a family of five.
The yard ended in a round passage into Wonder Street.

One benefit from living in this yard, was that out of the twelve children housed there six were roughly of an age to be pals, and, apart from the usual squabbles we all got on pretty well. When eventually the air raid shelters were built we quickly commandeered them as a Gang Hut. Fortunately they were never needed for anything else, as on the few occasions that air raids occurred, the neighbours seemed to congregate in our house. We kids enjoyed being put in the cupboards and far from fear, we enjoyed those times. I'm sure that any bombs that fell in our vicinity and some did, were left overs from raids on Liverpool or Manchester but one time a tree was set on fire by an incendiary at the end of our yard. That was the height of our blitz.

Over the wall from Simpson's buildings was Pilkington's yard, a coal merchant, who had two lorries and six horses all busy delivering coal. Great times were had in school holidays riding the horses down to the 20 acre field right at the end of Caldervale Road and enduring the long walk back. Long days were spent at the same field, haymaking, and riding there on flat carts. At the end of the day queuing at Pilkington's desk, for small wages but each given a bottle of pop, we never complained at the value.

The same Mr Pilkington, if he saw us hanging about with

nothing to do, would sometimes bring out an old coil of rope and pretend he had a job for us stretching it, so organised a tug of war. A kind man, always, who really loved horses and would never see one badly treated. On the sad day of his funeral, he was taken to the cemetery, his coffin on the back of a flower bedecked coal cart, pulled of course by one of his beloved horses.

Mrs Pilkington reminds me that there is a theory often proclaimed, that people eventually grow to look like their dogs, well Mrs Pilkington kept Pekinese and certainly gave credence to the truth of this. She also had a speech impediment, which when she spoke, produced a kind of yodel, and the dogs barked in much the same tone. A small lady, sort of blondish grey in colour who always appeared to be lit up in bright colours in spite of the drab surroundings of the home-cum-office. I am amazed that these thoughts can lie quietly at the back of one's mind for so long and never thought of for over 50 years and yet surface when the mind is focused.

Below the stables in that yard were four or five cottages some housing his workmen. One, Joe Schofield spent all his working days just filling and weighing hundredweight sacks of coal, I often awoke to the sound of Joe's awful voice singing some dirge that took his fancy. Another occupant a very ugly man with a deformed face would answer to Clark Gable, cruel wit.

At the end of this row an empty cottage was used throughout the war for the men of Wonder Street for fire watching. To raise money for blankets, stirrup pumps etc. Rabbit pie suppers were organised and held there, well attended and made into enjoyable nights. Pilkington's yard had a great influence on my childhood, for one thing you had to get up early if you wanted to spend the day riding round on the coal carts, and we all did.

4, SIMPSON'S BUILDINGS

It does not really matter whether we start at the bottom, or the top, cellar or attic of number 4, as all were the same, very damp. So, I'll work my way up. The cellar was at the bottom of an outside flight of stone steps, with a door on the right leading into a small coal cellar, served by a grate set into the yard. A door on the left led into the cellar itself. Just inside this door, on a high shelf, sat an electric meter, which we fed with pennies. To the left was a sash window, giving poor light, as it looked onto the outside stairs. Placed in front of this was a shallow stone sink leading to the large "set pot", which with it's brick surround filled the entire corner. Under this was a fire grate, to boil the water on wash days, when the whole house seemed to be full of steam.

The opposite corner held a floor to ceiling cupboard, which I'm sure, was never used because of the damp. The return wall led to the stairs, again, stone, up into the living room. This wall, for some reason had been graced with a dado height wainscoting which to me, seemed to be out of keeping with the surroundings.

At the times when the river Calder was in flood, it was not unusual for the waters to back up and flood the cellar. This happened on quite a few occasions but usually was short lived, apart from twice, when we had the flood for several days. This created a problem, as we were unable to feed either the gas or electric meters. The only solution was for my father to don his one piece bathing suit and looking like a latter day Captain Matthew Webb, strike out from the steps, with a mouth full of pennies, a very unpleasant task in the cold and filthy water.

The other occasion, I remember my friend Geoffrey (Minnie) Lovell and I decided to sail our large tin bath around the cellar, which seemed to be a very good idea at the time. So we set about capturing the bath, which was floating round at liberty. We at the bottom of the stairs with a weighted rope successfully hauled the craft to the bottom of the stairs, then began the struggle for who would be first in. Happily, I lost and Geoff got one foot in the bottom of the bath, which being so light, immediately moved off, dropping him into the swirling torrent, we decided that would be enough sailing for today.

Such were the joys of our cellar, even in the height of a hot summer; the stone floor never lost its black, wet look.

Accending the cellar steps, all stone and limewashed walls we reach the Cellar Head where was set a large keeping stone, on which everything to be kept cool was stored. These were the days long before domestic refrigerators and so regular daily shopping was necessary. I can remember my mother asking at virtually every house in the yard if anything was needed as she was "Going up street" which meant Kirkgate where all the multiples such as Gallons, Meadow Dairy etc. were situated. In these war days of course everyone was registered at certain shops, so could only buy rationed goods where they were registered.

Enter the living room, although we never called it that, as there was no need, it being the only one. There isn't much to say about this room, it held a two-seater settee and two easy chairs, also a square table and four chairs, a sink between the outside door to the yard and a sash window. On one wall was the fireplace with a combined oven and a place for a gas ring, all cooking was done there, I often wonder how. Either side of the fireplace were cupboards, one halfway, the other floor to ceiling, all very much used. Ironing after wash days was done the old fashioned way with two heavy flat irons, heated in turn on the fire and held by bits of blanket to protect the hands against burns. Tony and I saved our paper money (delivering) to buy our Mum a Morphy Richards electric iron as a surprise, she was overjoyed and it made life a bit easier. As there was only one electric plug in the house, it was plugged into the light socket, this made reading a practised art, with the light whirling round and round as she ironed away.

A corner door led to the bedroom stairs, the only bedroom, where the whole family slept. Tony and I in one double, mum and dad in the other, later when Peter arrived, he had a cot in the same room. This state of affairs was fine, and normal when we were children, but you will appreciate was embarrassing as we grew older. There was no way around this until such time as we were lucky enough to be given a council house or "When we get our key" as it was more popularly known. At this time, I had of an idea. There was an attic above, with a sloping roof and a skylight, which had always leaked in rainwater. The previous tenants to us had attempted to put a bed in there, but as the floor was partly rotten (under the skylight) the leg of the bed had gone through the floor, the proof of this being a patch on the bedroom ceiling below almost acting as a warning not to try again, hence my idea. I managed to obtain a number of tea chests and dismantled these to nail all over the floor, these were strong enough to support the furniture needed and with lino added and a few coats of distemper on the walls, we now had a second bedroom for Tony and I to sleep in.

These factors always weighed heavy with me, I found it hard to understand, that we didn't even own the roof over our own heads, but paid a man the princely sum of 9 shillings (45p) per week, for the privilege of living here. In hindsight of course, these were different days and we had to think ourselves lucky even to have this. I know this influenced my future thoughts regarding owning my own home, so some good did come out of it.

WONDER STREET

In 1963 the Grove area including Wonder Street was demolished, some would say not before time, and I would not disagree. Even so the place still had some very happy memories for me and so at the end of my days work on the Friday I took myself off to survey the scene. As I stood there, I was joined by Jimmy Kilkenny, who had lived in the adjoining Grove Street and was doing exactly the same as me and I well remember him saying, " where did we all live Terry?" It did seem amazing that all our neighbours had been housed in such a small area which seemed minute, now that all the houses were down. Now after forty years I wonder how many of them I remember. The shape of the street is still there, but new buildings have been erected to replace the old ones. The yard has disappeared totally and been replaced by a large building housing the business of my very good friend Gerry Booth.

On our side of the street starting at the Grove road end was the Grove Inn, then a tiny place, but much later extended. It was kept at that time by Mrs Hulme and next to it a small yard with two houses, one occupied by an ageing mother and daughter, whose name I never knew. The other housed the Pursegloves with two boys, Barry and Roger. Working down was the home of the Gunns with a side door into our yard, three sons Frank, Lawrence and my hero at that time Edward (Teddy). Lawrence later played on the wing for Featherstone Rovers. The other side of the passage was the Tollace family, with one son Charlie. The next was an unknown old man, with the Scarves, one son, Dennis and a sister. Next the Macrells Geoff and Eddie, (who also played for Featherstone Rovers) then Pilkingtons house with a side door into the yard already described. After the yard was a building, with many happy memories as it was rented by two great friends older than my brother and I, Les and Frank Harding, who kept show rabbits and guinea pigs and got up to all manner of things on it's two floors. We grew and sold mushrooms, and made and painted toys and wooden jigsaws. Upstairs we made ourselves a gym with mainly home made apparatus. Always something new to do and introduced us to the game of Monopoly which I couldn't wait to get the evening papers delivered to get involved in the game. To complete our side of the street were the Hoyles with one daughter Olga, one of only two families to own a car.

The other side presents more of a challenge, with broken spaces and old buildings, but I can remember a Mrs Robshaw and her son Ken, much older than we were. Then a row with the Welches the Colbecks, two boys and a girl, Mollie. The boys Roy who achieved very high rank in The RAF and Victor who I think got to be a Major in the Marine Commandos. Vic was younger than we were, but was always with us as part of our games, largely because he was brave enough to walk under the belly of one of Pilkingtons horses. The Colbecks were a very nice family and looked up to by their neighbours. Next came the Twiveys, who were involved in cattle transportation and had the other car in the street. With one daughter, Joan, very pretty and later to own and run with her husband Frank the Stoneleigh Hotel. At the very bottom of the street was the yard where Frank and Les lived, with another brother, John, serving in the Marines, then a strange concoction of houses in corners, up stairs,Dickensian in character, hard to place now but with another pal Bob Burns living in one.

One occasion not to be overlooked in the street was the party to celebrate V. E. Day. Everyone helped to decorate the street and brought out things that had been hoarded and saved throughout the war. Music was provided by the Colbecks, who had carried out their radiogram into the street for the dancing. Drinks were supplied of course from the Grove pub, which did a roaring trade. One small episode I remember well although I should not have been privy to it. Because of some connection that the Colbeck family had with the Town Hall and the mayor's charities, the present incumbent Harry Watson, also a prospective Conservative candidate for Parliament, turned up to the party, with his friend and next door neighbour Chief Constable Godden. As Harry Watson was chairman of the Watch Committee and the Chief Constable was answerable only to that, they formed a formidable but fair combination. At 10.30 Mrs Hulme called "time" and stopped serving drinks "Why have you stopped serving?" asked Mr Godden."Why because it is after time" said Mrs Hulme, out came the Chief Constable's notebook a brief scribble and drinking was able to continue unabated to crown a very happy and memorable night.

PETER

As adults we are aware about the dangers we can encounter even with day to day living. Consequently young children will never see danger. It is not that "Fools rush in" they are not even old enough to care.

I was nine years old when my mother told my brother and me that we were having a baby. When we told our friends the news, they already knew, because they said they had seen she was getting fat. I confess I knew nothing about it, I was happy to know that I was able to push the pram, and perhaps play stagecoaches. Perhaps it was a bribe. Anyway if Peter had known the things we were preparing, he would be best back in the womb.

Where we lived in the Grove, the roads were mostly cobbles. Except one, Charlotte Street, because it was a smooth tarmac road (named after Queen Charlotte, wife George III) and as children used it to play whip and top and racing Dinky cars. Peter was enjoying the ride in his pram and I pushed it as fast as I could into the main road, Kirkgate, trying to let the pram go itself. Tony was trying to stop it and I wanted to see how fast it would go before I had to brake. Anyway a woman saw what we were doing and told my parents. I am sure you will know the outcome, sorry, was not enough. Although the traffic was nothing like now, it was a foolish and dangerous thing to do.

Another time with a few pals, we were pushing Peter in his pushchair to see the floods on Thornes Lane. When we found Thornes Wharfe banking awash, we had to climb up onto the top of the wall, carrying Peter in the pushchair between two of us, with the river on one side and the rhubarb flooded fields on the other. We had to climb from the wharfe, to the "Chain Bridge" into Denby Dale Road. By this time it was getting dark. Even now I could shudder with just the thought of it. But it was nothing unusual to do these things, we certainly had charmed lives. Which just goes to prove my initial thought children do not recognise danger.

THE LOVELLS

Our next door neighbours at number 3 were the Lovells, with Harry Foster (Fos) the lodger I have already mentioned. Of the two boys, Geoff, being nearer my age was my friend and we spent time in each others houses. Mrs Lovell was prone to what my own mother called her "do's". I would think in hindsight, they were migraine attacks and quite severe but did not attract much sympathy from the household. On one such occasion I well remember I was playing next door, quietly, Mrs Lovell being laid out on the horsehair sofa, when Harry came in from work at Walton pit. These were the days before pit head baths and having a job on the "screens". He was just about jet black and took a seat in front of the open fire, whilst waiting for his bath water to heat. Enter Mr Lovell, a man of few words and dour countainance. "Shift Fos" he said. Harry stuttered his intention to hold his ground, whereupon Lovell decided to burn him away from the fire and spent the next half hour running up and down the cellar steps fetching buckets of coal and building up a great blaze. Harry, sweat pouring off him, stood his ground, Mrs Lovell sighed and moaned on the horsehair sofa and begged an end to the hostility. At this juncture, I took my leave and went home being quite used to such events, it gave me no surprise.

A regular feature of the Lovell's Sunday was the great debate about how much the "pop" had cost. One or other of the boys would set out on the bike to a shop in Kirkgate called the Bon Bon to collect an assortment of lemonade, dandelion and burdock and Tizer. The confusion as to cost was made worse because of the "empties" taken back from the week before, most having 3 pence back on return, but Tizer having 4 pence on it's "empties". The arguments would rage all day and my best pal Pat Mannion, delighted in calling round to hear the great debate, with saucers pressed up against the dividing wall, only one brick wide. Listening to the overbearing voice of Lovell, the whining of whoever had made the delivery that day pleading innocence and the laboured stuttering of Harry putting in his many "ttt'mans" and trying to be heard . Nothing was ever resolved but my great joy was to listen to the weekly episode. In those far off days, with cabaret next door, who needed television?

THE WEBBERS

We eventually lost our next door neighbour and shared toilet partner, the retired plumber "Mr Sam" Robinson, a quiet gentleman who had always kept us unfrozen. The house passed on to Mr and Mrs Webber, who as we said, kept themselves to themselves, but lent Simpsons Buildings a bit of class. He in raincoat and trilby, she, in close fitting blue velour, whilst we were more flat caps, bib and brace. They also carried briefcases, but for all that, as far as we knew, could have been Russian spies. Years later, when I grew up and took to drinking, I discovered him playing the piano in The Black Rock.

The Webber's house backed on to ours, fireplace to fireplace and cupboard to cupboard, with just the one brick width in between. I remember it was one Saturday when the banging started and went on all morning, my Dad sitting in his armchair next to the half cupboard, with the radio on top of it looking forward to the football match, which would be on the radio in the afternoon and complaining that he wouldn't be able to hear a thing if the banging continued. However, he needn't have worried, for round about lunch time, a voice out of our cupboard said "I'm through Mr Clarke".

Whereupon on opening the cupboard doors we beheld Mr Webber's head and shoulders inside our cupboard, "What are you doing in there" said my Dad. "I'm fitting a sink" said Webber, but we don't want a sink in our cupboard we cried, it was our refuge on air raid nights. It transpired the man hadn't realised the thinness of the dividing wall and the back of his cupboard, was the inside of ours, a sure case of intelligence without common sense.

THE CARLTON

I suppose the Carlton cinema was the main focus of our attention in those early years, I have long admitted that Hollywood dictated our fashions and to some extent our speech. The cinema was located on the corner of Grove Road and Grove Street, and changed it's program Mondays and Thursdays, with a Saturday matinee and later a separate Sunday show.

I will concentrate mainly on the matinee, which was the high point of our week, and we kids always observed a ritual before attending. Every Saturday lunch time, the Rington's Tea horse and carriage would make an appearance in the corner of our yard and have it's feed bag put on it's head, the driver of this combination having disappeared into one of the neighbours houses presumably to eat his own lunch. Later on a bucket of water would be produced and after a short pause came the climax. Out would unfold this enormous penis and a great flood of slightly yellow tinted urine would ensue, frothing about among the cobbled yard, not until the last bubble had disappeared, would we dash off to the Carlton. There was never a variation in this event that I can remember.

Directly opposite the Carlton was a small wooden shop named The Venture where we bought all our sweets and spent our meagre pocket money. It was owned and run by a man named Fred Mosby who was always Mr Mosby to us. I look back now and think what a truly risky venture it was, but at the time it was always called a "Gold Mine" by our parents.

Now the main event. In front of the screen was a long brass pole that carried a velvet curtain, to screen off what had been an orchestra pit. Every Saturday without fail, a cat would appear at one end of the pole and walk the whole length across it, which signalled the start of the programme, to great cheers from the young audience. I have never solved the mystery of the cat's behaviour. We would then have a feast of a cartoon followed by a comedy featuring maybe the Three Stooges, or Edgar Kennedy and then would come the serial, maybe a cowboy, or the all time favourite, Flash Gordon hopefully outwitting the evil Ming the Magnificent assisted by the beautiful Dale. The main feature would almost inevitably be a cowboy with Johnny Mack Brown, or maybe Tex Ritter, Roy Rogers, or Gene Autry and their faithful horses.

Throughout these proceedings, the noise would be tremendous with the cheers and the boo's of the audience, added to which was the never ending sound of the voice of Joe Corfield (Carlo Joe) shouting "keep quiet" and threatening to throw out any one who didn't. Joe took his job very seriously and looked like a Swiss admiral in his usher's uniform and flat peaked cap, always covered white in summer.

Years after the war ended, ice cream was introduced. It was Lyons and was delicious and even if we weren't at the performance, we would try and intercept the usherette in the foyer between circle and stalls to buy some.

As far as I can remember the Carlton was demolished along with the rest of the Grove around 1963, and with it, all those happy memories and fondly remembered heroes.

HEATH COMMON

One day, whilst musing about present day problems regarding friends who say it isn't safe to let children out of sight, I thought about my own childhood, and although living through the days of a world war, how safe we always felt and what freedom we enjoyed. Of course paedophiles, if paedophiles were there, were obviously keeping a very low profile.

Living where we did, at the Kirkgate end of Ings Road, it was as easy to spend our days either at the park, or at Heath Common, which usually won the decision being less tame than the park and having all kinds of diversions on the way.The group would be made up of eight or nine kids between the ages of eight/eleven all armed with bread and jam sandwiches (no butter), usually raspberry, which by the time of eating had crystallised into the surface of the bread but was devoured, just the same.

One such day I remember well, we crossed Kirkgate at the Crown Hotel and ran over towards the old bridge, calling on the way at a ruined and broken down shop, where we had once found cigarette cards fixed to a board. With the optimism of youth, hoping no doubt for a repeat find, alas not to be. From there we ran across the road to the "Old Man's Park" a small area on the site of the old town mill, which had been demolished to make way for the new bridge. This comprised of a grassed area with four benches and flowerbeds. As we explored the place, one of our number found what I now know to be a condom, but which at that time was a complete mystery to us. Various guesses were made as to its use, the favourite being advanced by Johnny Roberts, "That they fall from cow's teats and men like to find them and put them on their " willies". As one of the younger members of this group, it's uses were of no

Cricket pitch in front of Heath Hall.

interest to me, but it did seem a good thing to keep and so for the rest of the day, it was passed around to everyone in their turn.

Over the old bridge now and onto the "Skinners Fields" first examining the two water towers and playing at the water's edge. The next stop was always at the high bridge that spanned the canal locks, where we hoped to see coal barges entering the river, having been diverted around the new bridge weir. On again, over the canal bridge, passed the gamblers woods, where pitch and toss was played on Sundays.

Our way now took us up to Heath, with Dame Mary Bowles Tower, always to us a dungeon where in the old days prisoners were kept, not true of course. Next was Heath Old Hall, inhabited at this time by the army, in the form of a Searchlight

Unit and never suspecting that in a distant future I would come to live in it's converted outbuildings.

We had now arrived at our destination and as always spent our time in the old quarry, now long since filled in, we would tire ourselves out and with a final call at the "Whittling Well", to refill our water bottles and pull some water cress, for our mothers, (which they were never known to eat), it was time for home. Now the decision had to be made, do we go back by the way we came? Or do we go by the road, which gave us the added adventure of walking across the canal locks. The decision made we headed for home, worn out but happy.

This particular day did not end there though, our surprise find at the start of the day having been swung around in turn by all of us, the trophy finished up in the hands of Johnny Roberts, who together with his mum, visited all our homes to inform our parents what we had been up to and to warn us against picking things up "that could have been dropped by the Germans" and could have easily "blown off our hands". I was immediately convinced that she was correct and it was all down to Hitler. Men's willies indeed; much better to believe it was a bomb.

EUSTON

At last the time to pack our cases for our holiday to Euston, we had to walk to Ings Road and then across to Westgate Station. My dad carrying two big cases, and Tony and myself trying to carry small ones, very excited when especially we boarded the train. It was wartime. We were rarely fortunate to get seats. Now the change of stations, Grantham, Peterborough, March, Ely, Brandon, to Thetford, no corridor on some. At last to Thetford and Les Page's taxi. We really enjoyed this car, old leather and oil smells. All tired but happy.

My dad was a Suffolk man, the borders of Suffolk and Norfolk made Euston a Suffolk village. We were fortunate enough to go for holidays in my grandparent's house. The holiday was only one week of green fields and trees to climb and our "Townie" lives thought it was wonderful, it was like "The Darling Buds of May" even the time was right but in fact, it was August! We could swim in the river, it was cold, but warmed with playing, and we could dry out. I remember the ice-cream man had a motor bike and side car, I suspect this was just pre war, because rationing had not started. It was a leisurely time and the sun was always shining.

My grandmother's house was much bigger than ours, three bedrooms and a lounge, or parlour rarely used. The other thing I remember was a dark room where pickles and jams were stored, all home made. There were six houses, three and three on a right angle, in the middle, a pump outside for water, there was no piped water, gas or electricity. Each house had their own wood shed. At the back on a wooden bench were bowls of water for washing, always cold. Everything was spacious to me as a child and much grander then our tiny living room, one

Road through the village of Euston.

bedroom and an attic. I think the landed gentry owned the whole village, namely the Duke of Grafton of Euston Hall.

The A1088 road from Thetford to Fakenham spans the village of Euston. The Rushton Rd joined at Euston on a bend where all the houses were. Across the road was a coppice of elderly trees, strangely called the "Pond", I'm sure it had not seen water for years. It was round and fenced and it was a great place to climb trees. It was where our friends met. On the right of the road was a farm, apart from the farm buildings, there were only fields. On the left of the road our houses meandered to the old school, a post office and a collection of cottages, some thatched, most all white and when not white, then red brick with an infill of mortar and flint, something peculiar to Norfolk and Suffolk. The whole thing pleased my eye.
An unpretentious gate pierced the same mortar and flint walls,

at this time the cheap wooden five-barred gate sufficed, the iron gate having been requisitioned, because it was wartime. On then, to Euston Hall and it's church. The Hall and attendant buildings are the centre of the village, lots of people worked here and most of them worshipped here. At this time they were occupied by the Dr Barnados Boys. We always said the "Bananas" not to be unfeeling, but we were young and did not know any better.

I remember well the apple, pears and peaches and all produce from the gardens, my dad took us to see the head gardener, who he knew, and he arranged for a large box of apples to be sent on later.

The Hall was bigger as I remember it. Some of it was knocked down because of fire, and I remember seeing it over the broad water, which I think, was it's best aspect.

From 1767–1770 the Duke of Grafton was Prime Minister as a Whig. I think the present Duchess is Mistress of the Bed of Chamber to Queen Elizabeth II.

I have tried to describe the village scene, the buses were infrequent so we walked. Everyday to the home farm for milk, with a billy can about two miles, to Honington to see my dad's sister and four nieces and nephews, to Barnham to see another sister and four nieces about two miles, this particular road was very straight and tree lined. As I have said we were essentially townies and at that time my brother and I were about four or five years old, for me with my tiny legs I felt the road was unending. The grownups did not mind, they enjoyed the exercise, We had to see all the relations once a year.

But now the best part, playing with my friends, with new games and places to see, for instance, the war was not all bad. Some American P 38 planes based at Honington had extra fuel tanks strapped onto their wings and when empty were jettisoned, They were like a cigar shape, and our friends knew where to locate them. We had to roll the empty tanks, some times for miles to the river. They were wonderful kayaks when we cut them open by cutting with chisels and using rocks for ballast. All our games were home made.

One day swimming and playing about in the river, a long rope was found and fastened to a tree on the riverbank, and Tony and I myself said ah! "A Tarzan swing", I was surprised to hear my friends say, "What's that?" I thought everyone knew Tarzan. Because they rarely saw films in Thetford, they had not seen Tarzan. Then we had to tell them of his adventures, they were amazed, as if we had opened a key in a door. They were asking for more and we were happy to regale the exploits of Tarzan and also Flash Gordon, it was a fair exchange of experiences.

I think about August 1943 there were rumours about some manoeuvres. Suddenly, it came to pass. The Canadians and Poles were battling around our village, it was exciting and we were in the thick of it. We had a Sherman tank parked outside the "Pond" and it stayed there all night. People were giving tea and sandwiches to the Poles, and we children climbed all over it listening to the radio and handling their guns, we were absolutely riveted and would happily have seen it stay forever.

But too soon it was time to go back to our home. We had packed all our memories together into one week. It was a wonderful week and still had the pleasure of the oil and leather smell of Les Page's wonderful taxi on the drive to the station.

HEATH TO BARLBOROUGH

I had known the village of Heath as a young child and known of the legends of the Old Hall and it's tunnels.

I had in fact moved into the Heath Hall Courtyard in 1979, I was able to enjoy the ruins of the Old Hall.

About 1980, some people were working cutting down trees, the trunks were sliced to make name plates. I noticed a stump was loose, I was surprised to see a hole and when I bent down closer, I was amazed the hole was in fact a culvert, or small tunnel roofed over in stone, emerged from the bank. The stump had hidden the culvert for years, giving rise to the legend of an underground passage to St. Mary's chapel on the Chantry Bridge. Its purpose was to drain off the rainwater from the centre courtyard before it was roofed in. The north wall emerges towards the River Calder and had served as an emergency exit. These were Elizabethan times and dangerous.

About this time Margaret gave me a book of *Wakefield it's History and People*, by J. W. Walker and I learned that Heath had a twin in Barlborough Hall. The design of Barlborough Hall, Derbyshire, built in 1583, is about identical and must have been modelled on that of Heath Old Hall, though there were some modifications and variations, indeed the same mason's marks were evident.

Around about 1981, I had a change of job, a promotion; one of my responsibilities was supervising some merchandisers. I noticed that one of the girls had an address of Barlborough, I was curious enough to telephone to ask if Barlborough Hall still existed. I learned the Hall was there and that it was a prep school to Mount St. Mary's College. Armed with Walker's book and some other pictures, I proceeded to the Hall and boldly knocked on the door. The Headmaster was happy to show me around inside the school, for a half-hour, because it was lunchtime, but said I could spend as much time as I liked outside. Also he introduced me to Fr. McArdle who had written a book about Barlborough. With my Walker's book, I was able to fill in some gaps of information for Fr. McArdle. The upshot was an invitation to Heath Residents to visit on the occasion of the 400th anniversary of Barlborough Hall.

When I was able to report to the Residents they were happy to agree. There were no problems filling the coach for the unique trip. Older people remembered the Old Hall and the younger people were keen to see what it was like, prior to it's demise.

On the day everything was right, every part of the Hall, including the "Priest Hole" was inspected. The best thing we were all agreed on was with the view from the roof, it was spectacular. Buildings started the same, both had a centre court, but J. H. Smyth roofed Heath over with a skylight and staircase, about 1815, I noticed Barlborough had the same treatment.

All in all we had a very enjoyable time, giving our thanks from the Heath Residents, and especially to Fr. McArdle and the Headmaster, we then took our leave.

THE WIBLEY WOBLEYS

In 1954 Wakefield had a new Power Station, built on Heath Common. It meant things had to be moved, like the canal, which was filled in. There were other things which were moved namely the "Half Moon" fishing lake had to be drained, it was a beautiful place and deeply missed. Well! that was progress, I suppose. The drained lake was filled by thousands of tons of pulverised ash from the Power Station, which was coal powered. The ash was so fine it was like snuff.

Anyway the powers that be decided on a sequence of pipes from the Power Station along the River Calder and over it, bridging it by the "Blue Bridge". The ash was filled into barges and moved I know not where, as a result we now had a dry lake half full of pulverised ash. Over the years and the seasons, nature decided water would seep into the lake. On dry seasons, nothing, but if it were wet times the crust would lift up and the crust would undulate when we walked over it. Consequently the children ran over it and named it "The Wibleys Wobleys". I have experienced this myself and it was a strange feeling.

Our children in the Old Hall Courtyard were very happy playing in this magic place, sliding on the ice in winter and warming themselves in the summer. Thus it was on this bright morning when myself, Maxine and Matthew set the scene and decided to build a raft, lots of wood and rope at hand. Matthew was young and I was old enough to know better. After lunch we decided to try a double dose, but with the addition of the Hallorans girls, Kate and Sarah. Everything was fine, when the three children were sitting down on the raft and me pulling the rope. Then Matthew decided to stand up. The raft was not made secure enough to bounce up and down, consequently it fell apart and spilled the kids into the water, panic! I jumped into the water and grabbed the Hallorans and threw them up the bank, I knew Matthew could swim, and he got himself out. Well! Here we are all cold and wet through. I suppose it was half a mile, all up hill and with a child under each arm and Matthew and Maxine trotting behind me. I was tiring. The girls had lost their Wellingtons and I chastened and embarrassed. All in all it was an adventure not to repeated, but the girls, luckily, were adamant, I saved their lives.

MY STROKE

There was nothing different about the 8th of April 2002. For twenty years we had taken holidays in Spain, around the first two weeks in April and expected the same result. We were halfway through the holiday, as always, enjoying sunny days. But that Sunday the rain poured all day and so we decided to go to the Cellar Bar a favourite place to eat.

Monday was warm and sunny, so we relaxed with our books and stayed in the villa. The evening meal commenced about 7 o'clock, at once I knew something was wrong. But what? I could not hold anything in my hand and the salt pot fell over onto the table. I was unable to speak properly, no words

I don't remember any pain, just a hazy, slowly, nothingness. Later, I thought maybe I had a migraine, which is a similar feeling, I remember, I hoped so. Down to sleep.

Came the dawn! No doubt about it, I had had a stroke. No words, but I could walk. Margaret went to the telephone to call the doctor; it was cold, wet and dark. Luckily, the doctor spoke English. He confirmed the stroke, and rang for the ambulance.

I remember on the stretcher, it was raining and the ambulance man had difficulty pulling me up the steps, I was embarrassed.

The journey was about $1^1/_2$ hours, all I recollect was sounds of speed and siren and Spanish voices. Because I went headfirst into the ambulance I felt disoriented.

Next, the sequence from the ambulance to the stretcher, to the wheelchair, to the lift, to the bedroom, in which there were two beds. Now quickly again the sequence, to the wheelchair, back down in the lift, outside this time for the scan and back. Every word spoken in Spanish.

Now for the first time I recollect my thoughts. Margaret with me across the bed sitting in an armchair, all day and night. The other occupant was a Dutch man. He left the television on all the time, because I couldn't speak, I couldn't ask him to switch it off.

The days slipped into each other and I could not understand, or say simple words, therefore could not ask any questions. Margaret got some paper and made lists, I now could point to names and simples words and later, better with an alphabet.

After two days, Margaret moved to the Hotel, but I could not understand. The nights I spent looking for her up the corridors and stairs, but now unable to speak either Spanish or English, no one was able to help me. Some more tests. But good news, Maxine and Martin flew to Spain to join us, and happily the other occupant left.

The best part was when I was allowed to go to the Hotel. Then things were clear and I could understand and felt free outside the Hospital. But still restricted to call every day for treatment. Ten days after the stroke, I was able to fly home.

I felt all my problems were over, well, not yet. First I have the small matter of learning to speak again.

As I read my words, it is 11 months from my stroke. I know I have still got a lot of hard work ahead of me, but I will get there.

SPEAKABILITY

Of course I knew Ken Rollin as a rugby league player in the 50's. I didn't know him as a friend until May of 2002, when he came to see me in my home to talk about Speakability, he is the Chairman and started the group, Margaret and myself found we had an easy rapport with him. (Speakability is a charity organisation, which is a self-help group for people with aphasia.)

My first visit was to the Quaker House at Thornhill Street. I found it strange and at this time I questioned why I was here. I was new and I had a lot to learn about my own feelings.

After a while the visits were much better and I knew the group as friends. I remember I could not remember their names, so for instance Stan became "Stan the man", and it jogged my memory whenever I met him. I was especially delighted for Stan, because he knew all about mining and he took over the guide role when we visited the Mining Museum.

When the Speakability group went to Wakefield Golf Club, a man named Fred showed us how to paint. Having a small success myself with painting, Fred explained and showed me how to paint clouds and gave me some pointers.

The first time I met John Smithson, I liked him, he was amusing and he took me under his wing and we played snooker together at the Panther's Rugby Club. I remember especially at the Christmas party, he played his ukulele. I was pleased to get a copy of the book he wrote.

About a year ago it was suggested, I write about my stroke and to express my feelings in a painting (as shown on the back cover of this book). The pinnacle of my achievement was to present these to the Speakability Group at a meeting in October 2003. I am delighted to say I achieved that, a small thing but all positives.

STROKE-A-LIGHT

APHASIA ADVICE

Terry and Margaret Clarke

STROKE ADVICE

During a speech therapy session with Jo Richmond, she suggested I should try to write three pieces of advice I would give to someone who had just had a stroke now that I was two years into recovery. Having done this she said she was pleased with the result and asked me to try and do twenty pieces of advice. I said "no" it was too much, but as usual she won the argument and I started the task. The result of which a pamphlet was published.

1. If you are thinking about some item, try to visualise it.
2. Try to draw anything you are thinking about and keep it simple.
3. Because you have lost your speech, push the other senses harder, especially your sight, memorising every detail, any item.
4. Be aware that when you are tired you will find it even harder to speak.
5. Karaoke, You will be surprised, if you can read, then you can sing.
6. Photographs. With my brother, we looked at old photographs. I was delighted to know the recollections came back and we made a "Stepping Stones" moving on, also useful for communication.
7. Speaking. Don't be frightened to speak out, even if you choose the wrong words, remember that's what we are trying to achieve.
8. Do not smile needlessly. People will think you understand when you don't. Don't be frightened to say, "I do not understand".
9. A sense of humour is crucial, especially to laugh at yourself.

10. I had missed being able to sing. I found a couple of CD's of American Songbooks, by Rod Stewart and the words were published inside so I can sing along with the flow, it is especially useful for small words.

11. I know we all think fate was unkind to us, but retreating into a shell will compound the problem, we must look forward.

12. At first I could not make any sense of my stroke. Eventually, the fog cleared, it took time for me to relax, and this is the key along with deep sleep.

13. If you have a hobby so much the better. Anything you do to get outside of yourself has to be good.

14. It is as important to listen to other people talking, as it is yourself talking.

15. Keep the Speak Ability card handy.

16. If you enjoy films, ask the manager which part of auditorium you should sit, show your card.

17. When dining out, I find it is better with my back to the wall.

18. If you can read aloud, then you remember the words more clearly

19. Make a card and keep it handy. When the phone rings say, "My wife is out or one minute" You will feel in control.

20. Remember it's up to you whether you achieve a little or a lot.

MY INITIATION TO RUGBY LEAGUE

In May 1946 I was catching newts at Heath Common. I never knew, or cared about the Rugby League Final at Wembley; I was an eleven-year-old boy far too busy with my newts.

By the time I came home, I was amazed at the excitement. All my neighbours in the yard had their ears glued to the radio, (no TV then) and their excitement boiled over when Wakefield Trinity beat the mighty Wigan. I remember thinking I must be part of these celebrations.

I made sure my paper round finished as quickly as possible and made my way to Westgate Station to see the team bring the Cup home. Thousands of people cheered the team, who were on the top of a Beverley's beer lorry decorated red, blue and white, the Wakefield Trinity colours. I quickly adopted my new heroes and resolved Wakefield Trinity was my team. Rugby was in, newts were out.

Apart from a couple of Yorkshire Cups, the next fourteen years were pretty bleak, but I kept the faith.

Suddenly in 1960 we were in the final against Hull F.C. at Wembley. My friend Pat Mannion and myself decided to get tickets to go to the Rugby Challenge Final at Wembley in May. Having found our way to London, we took the tube to Wembley Stadium.

My first thought was, all Hull was there, the whole of the population and everyone decked out in black and white, all quite sure they would win. I recall quaking at the prospect.

Now we are out on the terraces, very warm, exciting,

Wakefield Trinity 1960. Ken Rollin kneeling on the right.

guardsmen marching, the bands playing, everyone joining the community singing with the conducting by the white suited Arthur Cager. Anyway the sun shone and I was determined to enjoy the experience win or lose.

When the players came out of the tunnel, the loudest cheer was heard and the players were presented to the Queen.

At last the kick off, one or two tackles against the Wakefield line and suddenly Ken Rollin did a side step, a dummy and he was clear of the try line. A long way to go and then the kick and the chase, he gathered up the ball, and scored the try within two minutes of the kick off.

I will never forget that moment and I suspect all who witnessed it will not either. It is still recognised as one of the top 10 tries ever recorded.

My fears were groundless as Wakefield won 38 to 5.

A DRASTIC TRIP TO "HANRATTY HOUSE"

After successfully travelling to Wembley and enjoying the experience of 1960 we were keen to try it again. Every May travelling by train, car or coach. We were sitting in Joe Gledhills, "Talbot and Falcon", when we were deciding on a future trip. Thus it was that the fated trip by coach was planned from Wakefield to Wembley to see the Challenge Cup of 1964 Wigan versus Hunslet.

There were plenty of takers and the seats were quickly filled, most were friends of long standing, and a sprinkling of new people. One of these new men was called Bob Cooper, he was keen to be the treasurer and we were happy with that. Although I must say, when I saw the accounts and cash totalled on the backs of cigarette packets and one time a blue sugar bag I should have had some misgivings. A local coach was to be driven by Bob's cousin, and we were assured it was "Brand New" with television, toilets, etc. and everything was of the best. That was the first of our disappointments. The second was that Kenny Peat, one of our number, had some lime in his eye and so he had to go to the Clayton Hospital to have it washed out with water. We were enjoying early drinks in The Talbot, so it was no problem. It was very early and still very dark.

By this time our "Super Duper" coach had arrived, it was ancient and not at all what we were promised. Also we had a new unknown driver, the storm clouds were gathering.

But fortified by a couple of Joe's pints we were still happy and started the drive down to London. Our driver announced loudly that he had to extinguish our reading lights because

"His battery was dickey". Dark journey, no lights, no toilets. There was the first murmuring of disquiet and the first saying of, " What a lousy trip"; it was to be our theme song. Eventually we drove into the "Blue Boar" for breakfast, we saw everything set out ready. But not for us! The management said, "We have never heard of you". " What a lousy trip".

Now we are entering Hendon, and on to the Edgware Road. " Where to now boss" said our driver, Bob said "Don't you know"? "I was only told to drive you to London" "What a lousy trip". There were cries of " Ring up Gillards". Of course the telephone box was across the road, one of the busiest roads in the world and it took ten minutes to cross it. Over the noise of the traffic, we heard Bob shouting "No change". A fusillade of tanners and bobs were thrown across the road to greet Bob's request. Eventually we learned we were staying at the Hotel Vienna, Maida Vale, "What a lousy trip".

We settled into the Hotel Vienna's dingy dining room and sorted out the bedrooms, I was rooming with John Lindley and it was passable, but some unfortunates were down in the cellars. Pat Costello and Paul Kitchen said the vibration shook the foundations when the tube trains pass by. We quickly got out into the fresh air and found an Angus Steak House. Fortified with steak and a couple of beers things were looking up. Now, some of the locals were asking where we were living, we told them the Hotel Vienna. They said "What? Hanrratty House" and told us that was where the police had found Hanrratty the A6 murderer.

We made our way to Whitechapel, enjoying a couple of old taverns of interest. About this time my our own problem started to show, I had a toothache. At first a small ache, and eventually really hurting. I tried the usual cures, but to no avail, it was spoiling my pleasure. The upshot was, I left my pals to go to the London Dental College, no joy, it was closed six million

Looking at the smiling faces the trip was not so lousy after all.

souls and no dentist. I made my way to the Imperial War Museum, where I had arranged to meet my friends. By this time it was time to get the tube to Wembley, and I watched the match with a fifth of Scotch swilling into the offending tooth.

Unfortunately I had no recollection of Saturday evening, we were very happy to depart the Hotel Vienna on Sunday and drive to north London, where we found a decent pub and had a good drink and some sandwiches. My toothache had abated, nodoubt, with all the Scotch I had consumed.

Thinking back 40 years and seeing what I have written it seems like only yesterday. I find something about the human spirit will make us change the negative to a positive.Over the years I find myself telling and retelling the stories, which become more amusing with the telling, the sad times forgotten. I know especially my friend Bob and the rest of my friends feel the same. So the trip was not so lousy after all!

THIS SPORTING LIFE

The Gods were looking kindly at Wakefield Trinity Rugby Football Club around about the 1960's. First they were successful to win the Rugby Challenge Cup three times, because of this they were asked to fly to South Africa and play in the inaugural Professional Rugby League tournament, in July 1962. The Wakefield Trinity team included some guest South African players, captained by Alan Skene.

When David Storey wrote his book and filmed *This Sporting Life*, for the character of Frank Machin, the early suggestion was Stanley Baker, as he was a Welshman and a Rugby player. Eventually a man I had never heard of, Richard Harris, was given the role.

At this time I was a rep. for McVities and a fellow colleague, Jim Higgs and I decided to watch the filming at Belle Vue .To form the crowd all the extras and Bingo players had been placed in the corner of the terrace, at the back of which was a line of cut out dummies all adorned with scarves and caps.

Jack Watson who was also starring in the film at the time when he and Elsie Tanner were lovers in Coronation Street. As Jack Watson passed by, Jim said jokingly "What were you doing kissing Elsie Tanner in the telephone box?"

Jack jumped down to the paddock, laughed and asked if we would like to have a part in the film. Some months later we received a letter to ask us to attend The Dolphin, in June, where the inside shots were to be filmed. Jim and I found ourselves just behind the "stars", where Tommy Fisher was the M.C. He was very nervous when he was making the introduc-

Cast of "This Sporting Life". Centre in white, Richard Harris and Jack Watson.

tions and said "Trinity" when he should have said "City" heroes. Time and time again we heard Lindsay Anderson, the director shout "Cut". When Richard Harris sang his song, very badly, the director told us to stand up and clap. That was the height of my film career.

I was enjoying the experience, but the part which I liked the best was when the old "Pot Man" disappeared, he was sulking because he did not get any of the free cigarettes. In consequence the whole of the filming stopped, all the stars had nothing to do because the scenes had been filmed and therefore continuity would have been lost. He was eventually found inside the bottle store, and dragged back kicking and screaming. While the production fell apart this man had kept himself busy putting the empty bottles into crates, I found this very amusing.

We were asked to sit one at the piano and the other at the

drums, so that they could do the lighting and camera angles, we were given half a quid extra. This made a grand total of £3 10s for the day, having spent £4 on food and refreshments.

Overall, The Rank Organisation was very fortunate that Wakefield and Wigan played each other for the Cup and the League and both games drew in crowds of 20,000 plus. It was these matches which were used in the film with Richard Harris super imposed as if playing.

RUGBY LEAGUE MEMORIES

There was never a secret about my love of Rugby League, indeed after the 1946 final I was hooked. I have fond memories of the humour of the people of the terraces, especially at Belle Vue. A few examples.

David Watkins was a brilliant stand off half when he decided to move to be a professional with Salford. At this time he held the record as the highest paid Rugby League player. David told this tale against himself as a guest speaker at the Wakefield Trinity ex-player's dinner at Painthorpe Country Club some years ago. Wakefield Trinity were playing at Salford. Harold Poynton was having the better of the duel at stand off and scored a try. A wag in the crowd shouted, "Can't you catch him Watkins". Later the same result and again the same voice from the crowd " Is he too fast for thi' Watkins". The third time with the same result and the same voice from the crowd. "Hit him with thi' wallet Watkins"

I was fortunate to know Don Fox as a friend outside the portals of Rugby League. For some years I had met him inside some of our favourite haunts, like the Wakefield Arms, The Redoubt and the Cross Keys to chat. But I have seen his genius many times at Belle Vue. One time stands out for me, a game in the 60's between Wakefield and Hunslet at Belle Vue. Don had a great game at loose forward and despite his efforts, Hunslet were rightly winning by one point. The referee was virtually putting the whistle into his mouth, when the ball came into Don's hands on the halfway line. I swear Don kicked the ball between the uprights, lying in a horizontal position. No doubt Trinity enjoyed winning pay because of Don Fox that day.

I was watching Wakefield Trinity, as Neil Fox was preparing to kick a crucial goal. A policeman, instead of keeping walking, as he should have done, decided he was going to stop to see the kick. Several spectators started shouting to move on, as they could not see the ball, the policeman stood his ground, to more calls of "Move on" and "Nay lad, move on". Having missed seeing the kick, the policeman then preceded on his walk. A friend of mine, Stan Cross, now shouted "Nay! Don't ask him to move on now, I want a cutting from him"

Wakefield were playing Wigan at Headingley and the whistle signalled the finish of the match, Wakefield had lost. As the players trooped off, one of our number, Don Grainger shouted "That was never a try Boston". Billy Boston said loudly to him,"Look at the papers tomorrow, and see whether or not it was a try."

TOMMY FISHER

I was never lucky to see " Sinatra at the Sands" or "Sammy Davis at the Flamingo", as much as I would have enjoyed it. But I was certainly lucky to see Tommy Fisher at The Dolphin, so I will be happy to the settle for that.

Tommy was the landlord of The Dolphin in the 1960's and for him variety was the spice of life, and he would try anything for a change.

I remember the Striptease craze, Tommy would throw himself into it with gusto. With the Dolphin and the London Music Hall near by in the Springs.Both booked in the same strippers, the girls moving back and forth between the two and the crowds of people following every time, running to get the best positions. Some times to ring the changes the girls were sitting in the bath on the stage. As a young man I found the whole scene very amusing.

Out of all his enterprises, I liked best when he borrowed a horse for a week. My friends told me about it and so I resolved to see it.

So Tommy hit on the idea to be a Red Indian Chief, complete with a horse, naked except for a loincloth, and a tremendous Indian war bonnet, with eagle feathers all down his back. Now Tommy was a small man, with a round fat body and apple like head, topped off with wire spectacles and with thin legs and arms. (You don't see many Red Indians wearing spectacles, when you think about it).

A small pony was stabled in the garage. Every performance the pony had to go from the kitchen through various rooms and into the concert room where Tommy, astride the pony, holding a bow and arrow, singing a medley of songs from "Rose Marie".

Tommy liked a bit of class, I notice the transom glass announced "Les Hommes" on the toilet door.

A couple of months later, I was sitting with Frank Hepworth and Tommy Fisher, drinking tea in Heppy's Café, when I asked Tommy "What made you decide to have a horse in The Dolphin?" He said to me "If I could have got an elephant through the kitchen, I would have been "Sabu". A typical Tommy response.

Over the years The Dolphin has had many names, e.g. Oh Boy Show, Wakefield Pride etc. but for me it will always be The Dolphin, and if you look at the façade, you will see it "Carved in Stone"

BILLY BROOK

I think it was in the early 1980's when I first met Billy Brooke, I know it was definitely around about Christmas, because I will never forget the conversation I heard then.

The conversation was between Billy and Jim Wilde in the Redoubt, where Jim was the landlord. Jim asked Billy if the carrier bag he had was full with Christmas food

Jim;   "What have you got in the bag Billy?"
Billy: "Cheese".
Jim: "Just cheese?" you like cheese then?
Billy: "No, the cheese is for the mice it's their Christmas too you know."

Billy liked nothing better than to make people smile, usually by joking. He would get their attention something like this:

"Would you like the droppings of Long John Silver's Parrot, genuine" or would you like Himmler's left finger prints?" All nonsense, but to Billy the more ridiculous the better.

For instance, I liked the story about his auntie's cat.

It seems the aunt died and left a thousand pounds in her will to look after the cat. After a while the money ran out. Billy rang the RSPCA to ask them to destroy the cat. The officer said he could collect, Billy had to bring the cat himself.

Not having a box, the cat was put into a birdcage and he set out to the RSPCA. Just then the postman came with a letter. The cat had won another thousand pounds on a Premium Bond.

So the cat stayed.

Billy was of portly stature, red faced, alert twinkling eyes. He was a soldier in the war and was a commando on 'D-Day' when he lost his wallet.

Having seen the film "THE LONGEST DAY" 17 times, Billy was convinced it was between John Wayne, Robert Mitchum or Henry Fonda who picked it up.

Sadly Billy died a couple years ago. I was at the funeral and so were many others. I remember that the priest made reference to how he loved a joke.

I am sure our lives our poorer without Billy Brook.

DOUGIE'S EULOGY

I have two immediate problems.

One, how do you say a few words about a giant?

And two, what new thing can I add to what you all already know about Dougie Mann?

Well, the one thing that never ceased to amaze me throughout our friendship, was the way he totally knew himself. The answer to questions asked or topics of conversations raised came instantly, never with, "I'll have to think about that one". As if he had already sorted out an opinion long before the topic was raised and I think he probably had. The opinions were really worth hearing, usually funny, sometimes outrageous, sometimes outrageously funny, but always worth hearing.

In my opinion, it's this total insight of himself that gave him great understanding of people, he didn't "Suffer fools gladly", but everybody got a hearing.

May I give an example? Many years ago in the Talbot (it was usually in the Talbot). Evil Kinevel was preparing to leap across the Grand Canyon on a motor bike. A chap came up to Doug and said "Whats tha' think of Evil Kinevel, Doug?" The answer was instant, "Owt bar work" said Doug. I have used that many times to illustrate his wit.

Dougie was generous to a fault, you had to race him to the bar and he usually won. But his greatest generosity, was his friendship. To be a pal of Dougie's was something to brag about, and people did, especially how long they had known him.

In The Redoubt with Dougie. Good times.

I met Dougie forty years ago, in the early sixties, although I had heard about him and Gordon, from friends, many here today, who had worked for and with them. It was in The Talbot, rained off and there's a chap holding forth on all manner of subjects. It was during that session that I made one of my better decisions, to make a mate of Dougie Mann and that opened up forty years of good times, knowledge, wit and humour. It's been like an Aladdin's Cave.

But, now the hard bit, how do we manage without him? I know already how hard it is for me, but I shudder to think what it must be like for Mavis and Tony, I've just lost a friend, they've lost a unique and loving husband and father. May I offer you both the advice I intend to take myself, to live with the memories, there are thousands of them and they're all great.

Dougie died on the 29 November 2001. At the request of Tony his son, I gave this eulogy at Dougie's funeral.

"A TRIBUTE TO HEPPY"

You will have noticed on the top of your order of service, that this is the celebration of the life of Frank Hepworth, well, I've got news for you. I've been celebrating Frank's life for most of mine and I guess that applies to most of you sitting there and what a life. It's touched us all in so many ways and each and every one will know when they first met Heppy, the day, and almost the hour.

In my own case, it was just before Christmas 1950. Some pals and I had called in the Ram Hotel for an under age drink, on our way to the Embassy Ballroom. We were having a good time, because it was Saturday, we had a few bob in our pockets and the company was good.

When the dark, dapper man entered, great haircut, D.A. at the back, Tony Curtis at the front, flicked the lid of the piano, pulled up a stool and sang the full sixty four verses of Eskimo Nell and others, well that put 1000% on my good time. I was hooked on Heppy for life.

I was asked to say a few words here today. In fact Frank asked me a couple of years ago. He said, "Will you say a few words at my funeral". I said "Yes". He said, "What will you say?" I said I'm not telling you, so today Frank, you will find out.

But what a task, the life of Frank Hepworth in a few words, and which Frank, the musician, the humorist, the family man or the worker for charity? Certainly we touch on the family man and Jean who was been absolutely marvellous these past eight weeks and especially during the ups and downs of the last two, when she never gave in to the last.

So in the main it's the entertainer and companion and it's been humour and laughs all the way. There are thousands of stories and many will be retold today, but I only have a few minutes.

There was the episode of the starting pistol, borrowed for some idea at Balne Club. In those days the Eastmoor bus queue was outside Frank's Café. "Toller" was inside, so Frank shot him. "Toller" over reacted and panicked the queue when he fell amongst them and Frank said he wouldn't get up. But the panic subsided when they saw who was firing the gun "its only Heppy" it's to be expected.

He liked a drink, you could say. One Sunday lunch time in the Talbot it was very busy, he looked at the bar, saw they were about four deep, he turned and walked out as far as the bus station phone box, he rang the pub, ordered his drink, walked back and it was waiting for him.

Some people came every week for 50 years to hear Frank and "The Bushmen" play. But there was one downside; the great fault was that they never had a programme. On the bandstand it was always "what's next" because nobody knew.

Frank, and that great man of letters and virtuoso of the washboard, David Milsom, decided to write a programme. One fine day, outside of "Heppy's", they took a table and two chairs and sat down with a litre of Baccardi, six bottles of coke, a jug of ice and an empty sheet of paper to write the order of the programme. Two hours later the Baccardi, the coke and the ice were empty, and so was the piece of paper.

Why spoil the habit of a lifetime!

A couple of years ago Jean, Frank and Margaret and myself

visited Graham and Evelyn in Canada, who gave us a great time in Ottawa. The four the of us went to Niagara Falls for three days. I could not get enough of it. I would go back time and time again. Frank asked what I was looking at, I said I had never seen so much water and I wanted to see it again. But he just wanted a drink, Niagara must wait.

Frank dispensed his own kind of magic, the humour and gaiety came through his life.

Thank you for the memories, Frank.

ROGER CROSS

Enter Roger Cross, whom I met in my home at Heath around early 1983, and occasionally saw in the Kings Arms.

Later his home was the Old School in Heath, this was around 1984. At that time he started the Heath and Kirkthorpe cricket matches. After a year I started playing cricket with him. Our friendship started at this time. I was still playing cricket at Heath until 1990, despite moving to Old Snydale in 1988. The day of the move was horrendous and we were absolutely whacked, we could not be bothered to cook anything so made do with fish and chips. In this melee, Roger and Lorna arrived with champagne (and 4 glasses), this lifted our spirits. The cork was on the fireplace for 15 years.

Over the years I enjoyed great times and good meals. He was a big man in any big company, (he would never tell me his weight), a very funny man and great humorist. I took great pleasure in introducing him to The Redoubt and its patrons and what a can of worms it produced. I was happy to join with Roger and some friends to go on a couple of visit to Ireland. Very happy times, lots of food and drink and occasionally a rugby match

I knew he was partial to the television series "Cheers" and I think at The Redoubt, he created "Cheers" in the small snug. He would start off some topic in all innocence, after a couple of drinks it would turn into a debating society. Once Roger said to me "It's easy to get a load of pals, all intelligent people who enjoy talking rubbish for hours". At this time Roger started his column "1st Base" which usually referred to somewhere

The last day of "Heppy's". Author, Heppy and Roger.

in middle England. For four years Thursdays was a "must", where people were happy to have a mention of themselves subjected to the Roger Cross style of humour. I myself was happy to read a couple of items of "1st Base", heavily disguised, "Boules Garden Party" and "Three of us in the canal".

It was a sad day when Bob Cockcroft signed of with the "Last Base" closing the column when Roger died on Thursday 22-12-94.

ROGER CROSS "BOULED OVER BY THE REAL THING..."

It's a funny old game, boules, and not least when it is played under floodlights in front of the sort of baying throng normally associated with Millwall F.C.

Or, if we are being brutally frank about the ugliness of the mood of these particular spectators, even Prime Minister's question time.

I mention this aspect of the affair only to acquaint readers with the dark side of great wealth and privilege, bearing in mind that what had been touted as a "simple boules party" was actually being held at a large country house deep in Middle Yorkshire. Like most owners of country estates, the occupants have obviously known better times, yet seem to be making a good fist of having to survive, humiliatingly, in what was once the gatehouse to the rolling parklands.

With a mere five bedrooms two bathrooms and 10 cars, they were doing their best, and for years, it seems, their summer boules party has seen the village en fete for weeks in eager anticipation.

Knowing this, and having been tipped off about the intensity of competition by a white-haired old retainer serving drinks who said he was the head gardener normally, I wasted no time in devising a cunning plan.

Yet at this point it is worth pointing out that I am not totally inexperienced where the business of participation in high-level gladiatorial sport is concerned, having jostled with hacks for the best seats in press-boxes at stadiums around the world.

And it can have fallen to few men to have left the bulls running through the streets of Pamplona, well, standing, simply by nipping up the stairs to a second floor balcony in the Plaza del Ayuntamiento 10 minutes before they were actually released.

Several of the Spanish locals, all hopelessly drunk and dressed in ludicrous white trousers and shirts and red kerchieves, seemed moved to shout up to us what is presumably the traditionally greeting for strangers, and handed down through the generations by Ernest Hemmingway in every book he wrote about bull-torturing: "Nada cojones, Inglesi!"

Whatever it means, the key to coping with sporting combat is all in the mind. It seems to work for them, which is why I heard myself whispering to each opponent at Saturday's boules-fest that, as anyone who had spent an hour at a hypermarket in Calais could tell them, what we were really playing was petanque.

Being invented by the French, of course, the game involves a minimum amount of skill while at the same time shamelessly favouring those with absolutely no scruples.

It also helps if you can cynically scatter everyone else's boules (by lobbing the silver orb in such a way that it descended vertically onto your opponents meticulously placed effort).

The estate workers, many of whom had been allowed to watch proceedings in front of the big house, didn't seem too impressed. But as I never tired of reminding them, it really is a funny old game, petanque.

YORKSHIRE POST, THURSDAY JULY 21 1994

ROGER CROSS: "A DROP OF THE WET STUFF..."

To all intents and purposes it was the usual, uneventful first few hours one tends to associate with arriving in Ireland: a parking ticket, a mollusc wedged in the windpipe, and three of us in the canal.

Acclimatisation over there is traditionally swift and often terrible, of course, and there is nothing worse than falling among friends within minutes of getting to Dublin.

The plan last Friday was to meet up in a city-centre hostelry, have a quick dustbin lid- sized plate of oysters (the person eating the fewest humiliatingly having to stay off the drink to be driver for the day) and then head for Galway 135 miles away. Things went as smooth as Guinness (£1.76 per pint) – apart from the near-fatality with the stubborn oyster in the unseemly haste to avoid sobriety, and the parking ticket— that is.

An hour west of Dublin, nature reared its head ugly and, miles from anywhere, it became imperative to find a toilet. In the absence of such, a deserted stretch of disused canal bank suitably shielded below a grassy knoll, seemed a happy compromise.

Until, that is, a hat blew off (and in) and we formed a chain to retrieve it as quickly as possible considering it was rapidly filling with brackish water and green slime.

Despite obeying strictly all Isaac Newton's laws concerning gravitational pull and the dynamics of kinetic energy, we were reminded within seconds of that most ancient truth of all (the one about chains being as strong as their weakest link, etc.).

After we had climbed out of the canal, and as hard as it is to concentrate with algae protruding from every nook and cranny, the general consensus appeared to be that I might just have been at fault, in my admittedly crucial role as "anchor", by inadvertently losing my footing and sweeping the rest of the chain to ignominy.

It is at moments like this that one wonders just how the English summon up the cheek to tell jokes about the Irish.

Be that as it may, we swept triumphantly into the ancient city of Galway in our boxer shorts, anxious to sample some of that mystical west coast Gaelic magic of song and legend.

We pulled outside one of the most famous traditional music pubs, down by the same harbour that remained so very loyal to Richard III's charter for 200 years until that nasty Oliver Cromwell arrived to punish them.

We pulled on our happily, by now, dry trousers and waited expectantly as a passing native obviously prepared to say something friendly in that liltingly intoxicating local patois, famously soft and gentle as a morning mist: "Ayup, are you daft buggers from Yorkshire then?"

By one of those coincidences so bizarre and extreme even Arthur C. Clark might reach for a stiff one, we had arrived at the pub on the one night of the year when the band of Irish foot-tappers was from...Wakefield!

This being a Galway still miffed about old Oliver C and his Roundheads, the locals know quite a bit about callous uncaring acts by politicians from a distant Westminster.

Which is why, when the band from an equally distant land dedicated an emotional rendition of the Canadian folk song "It's A Working Man I Am" to the distressed Yorkshire miners, there were some damp eyes among the tumultuous cheers. And then, just to remind everyone we were in Ireland, some local songsters bade "welcome" with, what else? "She's A Lassie From Lancashire."

YORKSHIRE POST THURSDAY SEPTEMBER 1994

H.M.S. WARRIOR (1860)

There was a problem living in the Old Hall Courtyard, the drawback was the television transmitter at Emley Moor, which was directly lined up with the Wakefield Power Station, and on occasions we received a distorted picture. The problem was resolved by tuning the television ariel to Tyne Tees, which meant we received their local news.

One evening I caught the back end of on announcement regarding the preservation of an old warship, which was in the region. I knew no more. What is it and where is it, I hadn't a clue.

On my frequent journeying to the North East, I enquired at all the places I had business, to no avail, no one had even heard of such a project. Because it was somewhere around the North East, none of my friends could help me.

Always having had a keen interest in ships, especially old ships my interest was aroused, but as time went by, I began to wonder if I had imagined the whole thing. On an impulse, I stopped in at the Tyne Bridge, where I knew there was a naval presence, Fisheries Protection, I think. Immediately, I had my questions answered, my old ship is H.M.S. Warrior, birthed in the Coal Dock at West Hartlepool. I quickly looked at my map and traced the A19, and drove down to West Hartlepool. It was easy to pick up the signs in the town and drove into the Coal Dock. I didn't know what I expected to see here, but it wasn't this dismasted hulk.

However taking a chance, I went aboard and wondered around. I wasn't challenged at all, maybe the workmen thought

HMS Warrior before restoration at West Hartlepool.

I was yet another prat from the Maritime Trust.

I suppose I was disappointed at first, because the ship was pretty beaten up, and about a century of grime had taken it's toll, but I thought to myself, you wanted to find it, so make the best of it.

This went on for several months, happily calling in to see the ship every couple of months, until one day I drove in to find a steel fence encompassing the dock from beyond the bow to the stern. I was cut off from my prize!

I think by now, they were somewhat used to my wanderings, because a workman came up to speak to me through the fence, explaining that only conducted tours were allowed because of the danger. He suggested I should to walk across to the Old Custom House and speak to Mrs Bartram the secretary, who would explain more.

HMS Warrior after restoration.

Having met Mrs Bartrum, I began to explain my position, she suddenly leaped out off the office, leaving me wondering what I had said. She was back in a couple of minutes to explain that she had managed to hold back a guided tour of apprentices, the guides being former naval personnel, and I would be welcome to join the tour. I was delighted to accept her kind offer.

For the first time I was able to know what I was looking at, some of the history and to know what part of the ship I was visiting.

After this visit, I returned to thank Mrs Bartram for her kindness, who gave me coffee, and suggested I might like to become a "Friend of the Warrior", I was very happy to pay the £5 fee to join. Shortly after I was surprised to receive through the post a selection of slides of The Warrior, a gift from this very nice lady.

I was now able to call on the Old Custom House, and know

how the ship was progressing and also receive the monthly edition of the "Warrior News".

At this time I became friendly with Mr Sam McClennon the Ship Master who would telephone me with anything of interest.

The "Friends of the Warrior" is a Hartlepool based organisation, established shortly after restoration work began on the Warrior. It is a registered charity consisting of volunteers who generally assisted with the restoration programme.

In September, Sam telephoned and told me on 25 September they would be "Stepping" the Mizzenmast and so I made my way to Hartlepool. I was amazed to see there were thousands of people. A giant crane was hoisted high and lowered to the 13 ton "tube". Radio, T.V. and newspapermen were gathering to record the event.

I could see everyone was very busy, so I accepted I would have to see the event from the dock. Luckily Sam saw me there and motioned to me to come aboard, and said "Get down to the lower deck" and I scrambled down and watched as the mizzenmast was lowered into the hole in the upper deck, through the main deck and into the lower deck. All this time I was trying to keep out of the way of the busy men. I could see that it was a highly complex and delicate operation. I saw a steel angle plate was helping to complete the operation, all the men were trying every thing they could think of to manoeuvre this tube. Suddenly a man said to me "Give us as a pound mate" I was delighted to agree and heard a satisfying clunk.

I had to go to work immediately now, but pausing to say a hello and thank you to Sam, who said, "Did you see it" I said. "See it? I stepped it" It was a satisfying day for all concerned. To see this 13 ton tube slotted through this hole, with only $1/4$ inch to spare each side was wonderful, yet to the casual observer it appeared to be simple and easy.

In March 1858 the news of the laying down of four French ironclads caused a naval scare in Parliament. The "La Gloire" was a wooden hull ship with iron plating. H.M.S. Warrior was the world's first iron hull ironclad, with her twin Black Prince. H.M.S.Warrior was launched at the Thames Iron Works, Blackwall. She was the world's first iron hulled and iron armoured warship. In 1861 the Black Prince was launched carbon copy of the Warrior.

1862	Warrior joined the Channel Squadron.
1871	Warrior was relegated to the countries reserve fleet.
1872	Warrior is taken out of service for a second slow refit at Portsmouth.
1875	Warrior is commissioned as a coast guardship at Portland
1881	She moved on for similar duties this time at Greenock.
1883	Warrior was obsolete. Just 23 years after entering the world in a wave of glory, the battleship had finished her life without ever firing a gun in anger Warrior was decommissioned and withdrawn from service.
1884	Warrior moved to Portsmouth where she lay until 1923.
1889-1900	Warrior still under the Admiralty is offered for sale. There were no buyers and she was removed from R.N. effective list.
1904	Ironclad joined the W.M.S. Vernon torpedo school at Portsmouth and became a floating workshop.
1924	Offered for sale again. No takers.
1929	The ship heads for Pembroke Dock Oil Fuel Depot near Milford Haven to begin her new

task in life as a floating jetty terminal. Started 50 years of ignominy, renamed Hulk C 77.

August 1979   Work begins on dredging the Coal Dock, Warrior's new home in Hartlepool. The Phoenix-like story is underway.

Sept 7 1979   Sea Shanties and civic dignitaries greet the arrival of H.M.S. Warrior at what will be her home for the next eight years.

March 1980   The Duke of Edinburgh visits H.M.S. Warrior.

Feb 1985   Warrior's two and half ton figurehead makes it's way from Portsmouth to Hartlepool to be fitted to the ship.

March 1986   The cameras come to Warrior. Blue Peter high-light the restoration work and all the ship's workers get a Blue Peter badge.

Nov 1986   The ships funnels 21 ft long steel tubes, are fitted on board using a heavy-duty crane.

June 12 1987   It's goodbye to Hartlepool, thousands gather to cheer Warrior on her way into the North Sea on the first stage of the journey to Portsmouth.

June 16 1987   Arrival in Portsmouth, and a place of honour in the Maritime Heritage Centre.

For my part, the Warrior was eventually a labour of love; the record shows the ship was so lucky not to be scrapped. Remembering that dirty dismasted hulk and now seeing her sparkling, new paint and everything all ship shape what a change.

I remember in the early days, the workforce at Hartlepool looked on it as just a job, over the months and years they became fiercely proud. I had the same pride with the ship, reflected in the bearing of my friends in the workforce.

Some years ago I was able to see the ship for myself and remember with pride the donations I gave to the Warrior

"Fore Topmast" and the Warrior " Gun Appeal". Very happy days.

I have one postscript. In 1997 when cruising around the South Atlantic, I was surprised to see a collection of paintings of the Warrior, one of which I had bought myself. The painting showed H.M.S. Warrior and H.M.S. Black Prince. The artist, John Wigston was on board giving a demonstration. When I told him I had bought a print, he said, "Thank you, after getting that commission I was able to give up my job and work as an artist full time".

HORATIO NELSON

I think Horatio Nelson without doubt was the most famous
character of history, in spite of his column, he was a tiny man.
It is difficult to think about Nelson without his ship H.M.S.

Victory, because of Trafalgar they will always be entertwined. It wasn't always so.

Nelson was born in Burnham Thorpe, Norfolk on September 29 1758, and was ten months of age when the Victory was built, in fact Victory was already an old and glorious ship when she fought at Trafalgar.

The young Nelson was only nine years old when his mother died and was only 12 when he went to sea as a midshipman. At a young age he was a Captain in 1793. He lost his eye in 1794 and 1797 he lost his right arm. In fact there was not much left of him to see. By 1797 he was a Rear Admiral and defeated the French at Abouker Bay. In 1801 he bombarded Copenhagen.

He could still find time to love Emma Hamilton.

When he was ordered to signal disengage, he put his blind eye to the telescope and said he could not see the signal.

His bravery was without question and because of what was to follow, we were safe in our island home.

After 1805 with the victory at Trafalgar and our fleet in tact there was no threat of Napoleon Bonapart. The next fleet action was not until 1916 at Jutland.

"This is the hour, this was the man".

THE POTATO CHIPPER

Some years ago, in the open market in Wakefield it was decided to open every Tuesday, and limit the wares to second hand only. It was very popular and very soon all the stalls were full of all manner of goods.

On the first day I decided to look around the stalls, I saw some fine books, all beautifully bound in leather, in blue, red and green, entitled "The Greatest Masterpieces of Russian Literature" Dostoevski, Tolstoy etc. Asking the price, I was delighted when the stallholder said £1, and as there were ten books, I passed over £10. "No! lad, just £3," said the stallholder apparently because there were three colours, so only £3, even a better bargain.

Some older ladies seeing this said "Eh, mister you could have kept them just for show". I could not help saying "There was a bonus for me I probably will read them as well".

I was so delighted with my purchasers, I was hooked with the second hand market for years and called not only atWakefield, but Leeds and Barnsley as well. Initially with books, all hardback and bound. Once I bought thirty-eight books by Dennis Wheatley in Leeds Market.

Then there was my glass period, coloured, cut, anything, biscuit barrels, pickles jars etc. Eventually went into Ginger Jars, when my wife Margaret said enough!

Enter the potato chipper. Do you remember how you felt when you missed out on something you would have liked to own? In my case it was usually an American car. I remember the chagrin if it was sold. Well! I felt the same way about this Chipper.

One day at the market I saw a small crowd of older people around a stall, so I decided to investigate. I could see the cause of the interest was a gleaming potato chipper, all sharp blades some flat, some crinkle cut. A wonderful thing. I must have it! But I was at the back of the crowd, I have no chance, there was too many of them. I could see my prize fading out of sight. One of their number asked, "What is it?"

The stallholder said it was a potato chipper and Army surplus. How much is it? The stallholder said £1. I must accept defeat graciously. "It's too much," said the spendthrift. I could not believe my luck "I'll have it!"I cried. The deal done, I sped off home with my prize.

The chipper would make short work of anything. It would destroy a cucumber in seconds. I remember I fancied some crisps one day, we used the chipper...wonderful crisps!

One day watching a television programme about food, to my surprise and delight I saw the only other one like it, the presenter said it would cost about £75 I was totally vindicated!

SANDAL CASTLE

All Yorkshire children, both boys and girls knew about the "Grand Old Duke of York" nursery rhyme, to sing or skip to with a rope. I prefer to believe the song is about Sandal Castle, rather than the son of George III, who commanded the English army in Flanders. In fact, he was a young man and there was no hill, hills are scarce in Flanders. As a Yorkshire child Sandal Castle was my playground, sledging in the snow, or fishing in the moat, and I totally believed the rhyme.

Around about 1961-62 I saw an item in the Wakefield Express, asking anyone interested in excavating Sandal Castle, to come to the Town Hall where a meeting chaired by Cr. J. Deen was to explain the history of the castle. As a young boy I was keen to see the castle dug up, possibly for the wrong reasons. Reasoning it was no good expecting other people to do the work, so I was resolved to help. Consequently I went to the meeting to ask how I could help. Obviously many people felt the same because the Town Hall was packed full of people interested in the Castle. It was not immediate because there were lots of things to do. Not least funding, but luckily there were people who cared and gave enough impetus to keep it on the boil, not least Cr. Deen and Town Clerk Mr Wylie, plus the leadership of Mr Phil Mayes and Mr Lawrence Butler as skilled excavators.

Eventually in 1964 the "the dig" commenced, the first spade was turned in the castle kitchens. But we had to wait a couple of weeks until the grass was stripped off. That was my time to move. I was too eager to start and just jumped onto the kitchen floor to hear Philip Mayes say "Don't move, you could spoil the medieval kitchen floor". That was my first lesson about

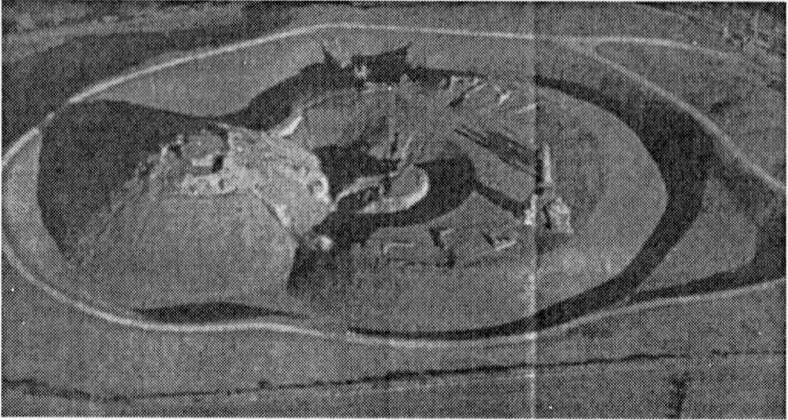

Sandal Castle.

archaeology, be careful with everything and especially your feet.

I enjoyed the experience and I felt had done some good for the two years 1964 and 1965. In time volunteer school children were able to go all day and so the evening was not as important. I was sure lots of children started enjoying an interest of archaeology because of Sandal Castle and kept this interest.

OLD SNYDALE

The first impression of The Lodge, Old Snydale in 1988 was not good. It was raining and the extension had a flat roof, it looked like a portacabin. All in all, it felt neglected and everything wanted doing, especially the central heating, which was coke and a bit messy. On our next visit we saw it had potential. I liked the outside inspite of it still being neglected. The only good thing about it was the space.

First we had to sell the Heath house, the offer we put in for The Lodge was accepted. I found myself more keen as spring came at last. There were two agents acting for the vendor, one in Wakefield and other from Leeds. Suddenly the vendor had a new offer and I thought we would lose the house. I had a telephone call from the Leeds agent who said "I am instructed you have to have this house" it was strange, and eventually we found ourselves buying The Lodge.

And now we have our house with a two and a half acre garden. From the first, I loved it and we set to with gusto. First we built an extension, large lounge and en suite bedroom overlooking the garden and got rid of the awful flat roof, putting overall a proper hipped roof. We started the footings on the 1st August 1988, we were sleeping there by Christmas. When we finished inside the extension building, painting, and plumbing, then we could relax for awhile. Before tackling the rest of the house.

Meanwhile in spring, and the following summer we started the immense job of taming our garden. Shrubs were now trees with neglect, and had to look at the leaves to identify which shrub was which. Every spare moment at the weekend was spent at this task. We would get tired and think enough is enough, time

The Lodge, Old Snydale.

to stop, but something would catch our eye, and on we would go again.

We had bought a second-hand lawn tractor and trailer ,without them, we could not function. What a revelation when we saw our lawns cut for the first time. Over the years with constant mowing the lawns got better and better until we had an 18 hole putting green and held a tournament, also boules parties which were enjoyed by our friends. I always said I never found cutting the lawns a chore, I could think about life and any problems.

We were rewarded by the birds who invaded our garden and wood. Jays, Woodpeckers, Robins, Finches (all) Blue Tits, Great Tits, Owls, Wrens, Wagtails (all) Gold crests Kingfishers, Cuckoos, Swifts and Herons which stole our goldfish. Also Rabbits, Hares, Foxes, Hedgehogs, Crested Newts, frogs, and two Roe Deer on our lawn. I had been told of the Roe Deer, without believing it, by a pal Dave Dey when we looked in the wood, he showed me tracks of Roe Deer. I was a disbeliever, but over the years in the Cross Keys other people said they had seen them, usually very early morning, farmers on the land, and once a friend Peter Watson rang and said "You have Roe Deer near your house" I suppose they were enjoying the young crops. In spite of all these sightings, I never saw them. When we had been living there twelve years, my wife Margaret saw what she thought was our dog, Tara, on the top lawn, but Tara was still in the house. Having heard her shout I looked up and looked out and was rewarded to see two small Roe Deer grazing on the lawn. Within an instant they were gone, their small, bobbing, white tails exiting their passing. It was a joy to see at last, I could now say I had seen Old Snydale's Roe Deer.

"Open House" was the order of the day for Christmas Night in The Lodge. The custom was to close after the lunch session in the Cross Keys and so many of our friends took advantage of the fact to join us. All in all the twelve years were happy ones until the time came to move on to pastures new.

THE CORPS CELEBRATION

"Report 24th March 1955 between10.00 hrs and 16.00"said the recall notice, telling me that my Queen and Country needs me. So foolishly I decided that meant exactly 16.00 hours. I reasoned they had got me for two years and no more.

Wrong! I was late for everything, uniform, haircut and lunch and I still had my blue "pick and pick" suit on when everyone was in khaki. On a black board a number 5506 said, " remember this number", which I immediately forgot. This was the most important number of the lot, my release date 5706.

This first day was the worst of my life, at 6.00 hrs I was tumbled into a cold, dark day of shouts and curses, with another twenty-four souls, and me still in my "pick and pick" blue, (the sergeants really loved this). This was the army, I thought, and I will have to put up it for two long years. There will be worst days and better days, overall it was good for me.

All though it was not my first choice, eventually I was proud to have the R.A.M.C. on my shoulder and learned about Esprit de Corps, especially when I learned we earned more Victoria Crosses than any other Regiment or Corps, and the only double V.C.'s.

Having finished all the usual "square bashing" in Church Crookham, I did a clerk course at Netley, Southampton, and then I was posted to Germany. I was an individual posting to Paderborn. I remember standing on the platform looking at the toilets, no one to ask which were gents or ladies, so I had to guess. I found myself desolate and very lonely for a few days, but I soon made some good pals, who stayed with me all my service.

'B' Company Royal Army Medical Corps, March 1955.

Bad Lippespringe was a village, and was the home of 30 Field Ambulance a small unit of about 100 men, which were often on the move, especially in the "scheme" season.

I remember it was in June when we had the Corps Week celebrations. We had a dance, sports and a trip to see the Mohnesee Dam. Apart from the Dam and a souvenir shop, there was nothing to see, and it was raining. One of my pals, Bill Lamb had already done this trip, and knew of and enjoyed a good Gasthaus, so the rain was no problem to us. Pausing only to know the time the coach would collect us, we made our rendezvous with our Gasthaus. I always enjoyed the German beer and my favourite food, "kotlet unt kotoffle". So good companions, good beer, and fine food, we were sure to have a good time. Our Gasthaus was raised up on the lakeside, with a wonderful view of the Dam. Our hosts were an older couple who told us, in their halting English about the night when the RAF released Barnes Wallace's bouncing bomb and talked about the strange lights shining across the water. My companions, Bill Lamb, "Yorkie" Cartwright, Jack Petrie, Ken Taphouse, "Lofty" Stone and "Brum" Rawlings, and eventually two others Riley and Muldoon decided to join us and enjoy the party. Later on we chartered a rowing boat, with this we were able to touch the rock wall of the Dam and see clearly the new stones to replace the bombing.

Having remembered the coach time was 4 o'clock we made our way to the rendezvous. Now things went pear shaped; no coach! For my sins, that week I had been promoted to full corporal, my friends were happy to remember responsibility carries with the stripes, so be it. We stayed for awhile, but we had literally "missed the bus". We picked up a service bus, roughly going towards Detmold. I saw a cream and red coach, lettered "Lippe Rhur Lines" and got off assuring myself it was ours. When we got around the corner, we saw dozens of similar coaches. There was nothing else to do but walk and we walked and walked for hours. As we were in civvies the few army trucks we saw would not stop. I had an idea, to ask if anyone was wearing army green cellar drawers, and to wave them in the air, so that the army trucks would stop. They were not convinced.

By this time it was getting dark, and we were seeing signs for Fort William Henry a Canadian regiment. I decided that there was nothing to do but to ask my Canadian friends for help. We presented ourselves to the guardroom and told our tale. Then the guard rang the commander and said "Sarge I have a load of limeys here, you know? a bunch of British". The upshot was we were given some blankets and we billeted in a corridor overnight. We were young enough, and tired enough for it not to matter.

The breakfast was very good, good food and coffee. I was able to speak on the telephone to our R.S.M. to explain what had

The happy wanderers somewhere in Germany.

happened and to ask him to get the one tonner truck. He rang back to tell me no chance of getting the one tonner, we had to sort it out ourselves.

Having seen the map on the wall in the orderly room, I decided to walk to Detmold, because we were short of money. So thanks to Princess Patricia's Light Infantry of Canada we set out early in the morning. We walked all day and arrived at Detmold. All of a sudden the pair Muldoon and Riley admitted they had money and paid the fare for us on the tram to Bad Libbspringe and then walked to our camp.

Apart from one or two references to the song "The Happy Wanderers" we were very tired but we were fine. Of course we were officially AWOL for one day, but Lt. Sayle the Company Officer scrubbed the charge, after I explained we had made the most of a miserable day, and the coach had left early. Any way it was my story and I am sticking to it.

MAXINE

I always intended telling you what I thought about things, at that time you were too young, and anyway I was sure I had plenty of time, nothing desperate to deal with.

First things first, babies, well, sadly no babies. Adoption, a big word and even a bigger step to take, but we took it. There had been thoughts of it, but now we had to think about it in depth. As we were Catholic, we first contacted the Catholic Adoption Society. A lot of things to wade through, especially with the Church. Throughout we kept in touch with the Adoption Society.

As in any birth you have nine months to think about it, but with adoption we didn't know how many months or even years we would have to wait. In fact it took about two years. You Maxine were blithely unaware!

But my problem was my head. I know I was for it, but I was troubled inside myself because I expected more and I was hoping it would resolve itself.

At this time Shirley was a secretary working at Marsden Fashions in Leeds, I remember she brought home baby clothes samples .One dress had a motif of a train where the wheels were buttons sewed on. At last some stirrings of pleasure.

Came the day I was hoping my first sight of you would be a revelation, well, not quite, but I was again expecting and hoping for more, I think we had about three weeks to wait until the six weeks period was up.

I remember getting up and trying to clear my mind about how

I felt about things. I thought this child would be with me for the rest of my life, so why do I not feel more emotion? But nothing, not even panic! Eventually we drove to Leeds and we could see the other children. Now you are there, my daughter. Shirley was lit up like a Christmas tree, obviously no problem there. I noticed the infant child had dappled legs, still nothing! Then someone suggested I held Maxine, I think it was the Social Worker. Even then nothing, not even panic. Then you gripped and squeezed my finger so tightly, I feel it still. In that moment you captured me for life. This was my miracle. This tiny mite released so many emotions I could not begin to explain!

In the intervening thirty-six years, all my secret fears came to nought, it must be the quickest bonding between a daughter and father on record.

MATTHEW

There was no mystery about my son Matthew, we had been eagerly waiting about two years for his adoption. We had a choice, so he was to be a boy and his name Matthew.

I can remember every detail of your arrival, I thought you looked a bit scrawny, but you quickly grew. I remember there was a discussion with the Health Visitor about a nappy rash, so after leaving the Adoption Society, we had a detour to Leeds to call on one of my chemist friend's, a friend I knew well, so you were assured of first class service. After that you thrived. I never once heard you address me "father", you always said "My Dad". I was pleased to hear this.

You never seemed a baby, although I knew you were a baby, but it could have been my fault encouraging your development. I am sure it is a very good thing for children to swim, you didn't need urging you loved the water and you never had any fear of it at all. Before you were a year old you swam the length of the Leeds baths, with arm bands and me swimming around about you. Needless to say, I was a very proud man.

As you grew you were keen to watch the " The Man from Atlantis" on T.V. and you copied him, you were like an otter and so supple, it was a joy for me to watch. There was a time when you wanted a badge for a length of the baths, we asked the attendant if he would watch the swim, I said you will only swim under water, the attendant said " If he wanted the badge, he would have to swim it on the top". You got your badge.

On Saturdays we always went swimming with changing venues and uncle Tony was always in attendance. Most of the time we called at Heppy's for fish and chips. Matthew loved "Uncle Heppy's" onion rings, your name for Frank. Saturdays were "Red Letter Days" with swimming, fish and chips lunch and games and playing with Frank's giant Great Dane, Khan.

To say you were busy, was an under statement. I can remember when friends called, their first words were usually "Is he any quieter?" You wanted always to know "why", so I would try to answer the questions. You must have decided to find out how dark it was in my car boot, and you locked yourself inside. Maxine ran inside the house and said " Matthew has locked himself in the car boot" I said " Not to worry, open the lock with the key and get him out" she said " He has kept the key with him" Now we have a problem. Matthew is screaming " Get me out "; his granddad wanted to drive a pick through the boot, to get air to him. Thankfully we prized the boot lid and you to could slip the keys outside, panic over. There were many episodes like these. You wanted to know.

I was not surprised to see cars were part of your life, you loved cars. You bought and spent years renovating a jeep. I have seen the result, it gleamed like new. I gave you my cherished "Jeep Manual" which I know you will also cherish.

My proudest memory is your Wedding Day you were totally self assured, obviously happy with life and contented. Still busy, but then, you were always busy!